DESIGN IN EVIL

DESIGN IN EVIL

RUFUS KING

WILDSIDE PRESS

CHAPTER 1

Miriam put on her last good hat. She looked at her watch. It was four o'clock. The drive to the subway would take thirty minutes, with a couple more to park the car in Harry's lot. Twenty minutes, then, to midtown Manhattan. That left eight for the walk to the Serbian Room.

Floyd would be on time. It was the worst of his habits. Nobody else would dream of showing up before six. The minor writer for whom the exploitation shindig was being given would be on hand of course, buttressed by his agent. He would already be a little tight in defense against an attack of nerves. The agent (male or female) would be svelte. Morning coat, if male; Hattie Carnegie, if not.

And Floyd, Miriam reflected, would be Floyd.

Floyd Meddleby was the literary critic of a trade magazine that had sufficient national circulation to put him on the invitation lists. He was a thin-haired, lank young man with kind brown eyes and what he hoped was an acid tongue. He knew almost everybody and, naturally, everything that was said about them. He could cover a cocktail party with a casual eye and label most of the celebrities instantly with their reputed vices. He took a good deal of pride in joining vanguards, no matter of what.

Miriam thought as she smoothed on gloves that Floyd was on the edge of asking her to marry him. She let herself out of the miserable little house and locked its door. It and its neighboring horrors were waiting desolately for the wreckers, which was how she had been able to rent it for a pittance on a month-to-month basis. The understanding was that at the first wave of a wrecking bar, out she went. She exchanged a gloomy look with one of the Fiorellis' hens and got her flivver out of the garage.

Floyd occupied her thoughts as she drove to the subway. Floyd as a husband. It was pretty cold-blooded, this doping out about your life's mate. Silly phrase nowadays with so many marriages tending toward a week-end basis. Miriam did not want that. She wanted it to stick. The thing was, would it stick with Floyd? He fancied himself hugely as a Lothario, probably (Miriam thought) without the lightest foundation in fact and certainly not with the cut for it. But if you let him have his little acids he was comfortable. And nice.

Miriam had met Floyd several months ago during her last job, when she had been a receptionist at a woman's magazine, the *Bazaar*. Floyd had obviously considered her a nobody, but a lovely one. She knew that. And he had occasionally relieved the deadly hopelessness and monotony of her penurious existence with pleasant and unimportant parties. She felt that she still meant little more to him than a facade that he wanted, but he had come to mean a good deal to her. Security, mostly. Security of a sort.

Otherwise Miriam faced that petrifying existence which had been filled in her mother's day by certain governesses who were accurately referred to as ladies in reduced circumstances. Reduced hell. She was flat. It was a choice between Floyd (whom she really liked) or a Mrs. Murcheson with her correct and expensive stationery and her "backward" little girl who would probably turn out to be a truffle-stuffed bad dumpling.

The job with Mrs. Murcheson was on the fire. So far there had been nothing beyond a correspondence following Miriam's initial letter in answer to Mrs. Murcheson's advertisement in the *Times*, but an interview had been arranged for tonight. Miriam decided it was up to Floyd. If he threw a ring at her, all right. A wire would cancel the Murcheson interview. If he didn't, she could start right in to fade as, in her mother's day, impoverished gentlewomen infallibly did. A fade a day. It had gone with the job.

Miriam parked the car at Harry's and took the subway. She looked anything but subway. It was a good hat.

Floyd was waiting in the hotel lobby. He was well under sail from three martinis and several highballs downed at a luncheon with one of his organ's most important associates, a blonde and statuesque Miss Myrna Marble, who leavened the magazine's surfeit of technical articles with a column called Trade Yokes, the content of which admirably lived up to its name.

"Miriam, you're very elegant. You look like a pincer movement or a panzer putsch."

"Make up your mind, please. Where did you get your start?"

"With the Marble calliope at lunch. I've told you about her. She's the Venus with all of her arms. Let's stop at the bar and you can catch up."

"Just one."

They went into the bar and sat down at a table. Floyd ordered martinis. He nodded expertly to one play broker in tweeds, to a juvenile in tweeds from a new Shubert revue, to a male gossip in tweeds, and to a casehardened woman in mink.

He said with considerable satisfaction, "Everybody is wondering who you are."

"Let's keep it our secret, shall we?"

Floyd eyed her critically.

"You do look something like Ann Sheridan. Something."

"Thank you."

"Don't be meek. I won't let you loose again among the *haute monde* if you do."

"What did you have for lunch besides lipstick?"

"Really? Where?"

"On your chin. You must have ducked."

He was enchanted. He borrowed her mirror. He wiped the lipstick off.

"She threw me in the taxicab."

"Has she got any belts?"

"Light heavyweight championship of the eastern division. It's my fate. I do something to them."

"I know. They take one look and go stark raving mad."

"You don't."

"I'm not the type. I'm a good old steady girl. Floyd, do I look as though I were beginning to fade?"

"What are you talking about?"

"Look at me."

"I am looking at you."

"Well?"

"What is this? Vapors?"

"I'm thinking of taking a job."

"What job?"

"Governess to a backward brat."

"Silliest thing I ever heard of in my life."

"I'd be very well fed. I'd probably get to work on the little beast's I.Q. aboard a yacht. Fancy me—moonlight on the fantail."

"Yachts don't have fantails. A fantail is a sort of poop. It sticks out of the back of a boat like a duck's bill."

"I adore being disillusioned. Now I want you to explain Santa Claus."

"You aren't serious about this governess business, are you?"

"My bank balance is."

"I must say you don't look it."

"Oh, you know us Lakes—while there's a rag left."

"Look here, Miriam, what's to stop you from moving in?"

"Is this a proposal or a proposition?"

"Be serious."

"I am serious."

"Then don't try to live up to your looks by being dumb. What's marriage? It's a handicap from the start. It's a novelty for kids."

"I see. But for us relics—"

"That's right. No locks on the door. None of this feeling I'm stuck. Hooked. We're both free agents. You've got no folks. I haven't. So there isn't even that. I mean, it isn't as if we would be hurting anybody. How about it?"

Miriam stood up.

"I think I'll go home, Floyd." She picked up her bag. She put her cigarette case in it and was conscious of the three letters in it too: replies from Mrs. Murcheson, the third of which had made the appointment for tonight. "I'm not being a prude. I suppose I am, really. It's a good word."

"Oh, for God's sake."

"Well—good-by, Floyd."

She left him sitting there gloomily looking down at his drink. Fog had fallen over the city, and a sense of foreboding was added to her deep melancholy as she hurried through the streets toward the subway. A foreboding of the future. A succession of Mrs. Murchesons seemed to stretch out into an arid spinsterhood.

Miriam retrieved the flivver from Harry's and drove through misted evening twilight. She reached home, or rather where it once had been. The house had been burned to the ground. There was enough light left to see the charred timbers and the chimney, which pointed a gaunt finger into the shrouded night sky.

More than the house had been burned, Miriam thought. Her bridges were burned too. The small treasures of her far happier early days were gone in the ruins. The little keepsakes that had meant her father and her mother, the few articles of fine old furniture that she had managed to salvage from their home on Murray Hill. Tears scalded her eyes.

She considered it futile to go to the Fiorellis and ask what had happened. There was nothing they could add. Nothing was left her but the car and Mrs. Murcheson. She looked in her bag and found three dollar bills and some change. She could sell Harry the car. The appointment with Mrs. Murcheson was for half-past eight aboard the yacht, which was docked in the East River. If she failed to get the job, the money from the car would cover expenses in the city.

Miriam drove back to Harry's. He was a thickset grinning ape of a happy young Irishman.

She asked, "How much will you give me for this handsome car?"

Harry looked it over.

"Thirty-five bucks."

CHAPTER 2

The man coming out of the fog was oddly courteous. Solicitous almost (Miriam thought) as though she were eggs. He looked virilely damp, not soggy, with beads of moisture sharply glistening beneath the dock's glaring floodlight as he moved in from the outer murk and joined her. Carefully. Stopping at a certain nearness.

"Miss Miriam Lake?"

"Yes."

"I'm Will Stone. The tender is at the landing stage."

"Tender?"

"We're lying out in stream."

"I understood from Mrs. Murcheson's letter that you were docked."

"We were. Look here, put this on, won't you? There is a chill on the river, and the fog—"

He ended vaguely, and took off a light slicker. She let him put it about her shoulders. She supposed it was a rebound from the cold, helpless sense of deep loneliness that possessed her, but the light, sure touch of his hand was electrically human and helped her out of that castoff feeling. Somebody—he—did want her to be comfortable. He wanted the slicker to shelter her from damp. It was all very warming.

Stone herded her through moist darkness across planking, under which slapped the restless river, and the smell was there, as always, of overdone snails when they're labeled *escargots* and cooked the French way. Ghastly, unless you liked them.

Miriam said, "I always think of snails. More so in ferry slips than here."

"You mean the smell?"

"Yes. I never could understand people who reach a water front and breathe deeply and say, 'Ah!' It's usually neglected lobster pots."

"And very dead fish."

"Or attar of kelp."

"I would hold the rail if I were you, Miss Lake. The ladder is slippery. I will go first."

Stone bulked before her going down the ladder that rose gently and fell gently with the movement of the river, and a duet of foghorns was sullenly impatient, blatting at them through the fog's trailing curtains. Miriam felt warmer and infinitely secure without the slightest justification beyond her great need for feeling so. A flash contrasted Floyd in her mind with this man Stone. Floyd would be lost among the darkness and the river sounds and fog. Lost with all the annoyed amazements of a cat dropped suddenly in strange surroundings. His little acids might even extend to a hiss and spit.

A tender gleamed pale white, and the strong hand of a sailor helped Miriam into the cockpit. She thought he looked at her with a grave concern, and his "Take it easy, miss" had the hushed quality reserved for expensive sickrooms. His muscular wrist had certainly been tattooed with an ultramarine monkey. An escapist, Miriam decided, from top-shaped women wound around with snakes.

Stone joined her on the deep leather-cushioned seat, sitting formally, almost on edge, and with no lounging comfort. Miriam looked at him openly from this nearness and liked his lean, reserved face. The fenced-in sort that dared you to find the gate.

"Is it far?" she asked.

Stone nodded through the fog. He relaxed a little and drew a pipe half out of a pocket and then shoved it back again.

"Why don't you?"

"But don't you mind? I thought—"

"Of course I don't mind smoking. Is there anyone left who does? What gave you the idea?"

"Nothing."

Stone thought: Now that's damn queer. But he didn't smoke. He sat up more formally, with his whole body held in a guarded manner. He studied Miriam covertly. His experiences with women had been entirely abstract and of the most professional nature. If you excepted, of course, Elsa Davis, who had created a profound upheaval in his life at the age of fourteen. He had gone to the limit of sending her a valentine. It had been a pink, lacy thing and definitely marked the end of his frivolities. Elsa was married now to a department store in Chicago.

This current specimen, Miriam, vaguely disturbed Stone.

He had found her instantly upsetting, and he resented the fact as a distortion to the cold, calm clarity with which he desired to observe her. There was little sound to the tender's motor, and fog muffled it further. Manhattan's sky line was a muted glow. Brooklyn's a duller one.

"This is something like living," Miriam said.

"Why?"

"Because it's strange. It's a relief from the normal. My own normal happens to be a particularly taupe one. This whole effect is theatrically unreal, like that show of last year where two men fished in the bay and planned murder, and yet the scene felt real. That's rather confusing."

"But surely you've struck this sort of weather before?"

"Not en route to yachts, Mr. Stone."

Stone said after a while, "Oh." Then he lapsed into a brooding silence from the shelter of which he continued to regard her covertly. He thought: I wonder if she's warm enough? Silly outfit to wear on a night like this. And why so eager? She's got a glow. Funny little thing. Got butter on her paws.

"Have you something on your mind?" Miriam asked.

"Me?" Stone added with hurried emphasis, "No, Miss Lake. Not a thing."

"You seem distrait. It's a word I love, and I'm always delighted when a chance comes along to use it."

Stone almost smiled.

"Distrait in a fog?"

"What's a fog to stop it?"

Speed slackened, and a white wall slid alongside and towered. Portholes showed orange blurs, and the sound grew stronger of an excellent recording of Beethoven's "Fifth."

"Well, we're here, Miss Lake."

"She's big, isn't she?"

"About the fourth, I think, in the country. She is the largest private yacht now in commission since the others were turned over to the government."

An officer was standing on deck at the head of the ladder. A sturdy, elderly man. Miriam thought: He looks like a hard-bitten father. He'd spare nothing to prevent spoiling the child.

His voice was shockingly pleasant.

"Glad you're aboard, Miss Lake."

"Thank you."

"I am Captain Liggett."

"How do you do, Captain?"

Miriam offered her hand. He held it fleetingly in his broad palm and then let it drift away like a petal.

"I hope you will find things agreeable."

"I doubt whether I shall be here longer than a quarter of an hour or so, Captain."

"Of course. I am so stupid about some things. There are many phases of life which confuse me. I forget."

Stone said with quick sharpness, "The saloon is along here, Miss Lake."

"Thank you. Good-by, Captain Liggett."

Liggett did not answer her but turned abruptly and walked along the deck in a direction opposite from theirs. Beethoven's "Fifth" grew stronger and swelled as Stone opened a door and they stepped across the raised sill into a stunning room.

It looked to Miriam like the work of Manson Interiors, Inc. It was empty except for the music which filled it from an Empire case above which a magnificent marine had been paneled into the wall. The marine resembled that new woman's work people were going so crazy about. Ethel Lawton. It showed no sea that you ever saw, but it did move and it was wet, offering its own peculiar restlessness beneath clouds that were lightly poached eggs.

Miriam said to Stone hesitantly, "Mrs. Murcheson?"

He stood by a chair, almost willing her to sit in it.

"Sit down, won't you? I'll let—I will announce you, Miss Lake."

Miriam handed him his slicker.

"Thank you for this."

"Not at all."

Miriam sat, and he left her, stepping carefully upon a Nile-toned carpet, and fog came in lazily as the deck door opened and closed. The music stopped and a moment held crushing silence while a record automatically changed. Not silence really, as foghorns again grew important from a distance and the tide run whispered as the yacht itself seemed to shiver with dim sounds of complaint.

Miriam speculatively observed a blank, fog-beaded porthole. She thought: All it needs is a face in it. Then according to the best horror authorities I scream. That Stone man, that very nice Stone man rushes in, and I mutter: "*A face!*" whereupon he hits the deck and there's nothing there. She idly pondered on what happened to all of the faces-in-windows that never were there (a fate like the reverse of used razor blades which always were there) and the successive record of Beethoven's "Fifth" swung out and stopped her from going that kind of nuts.

Miriam wondered what Mrs. Murcheson would be like. Her letters had been cordially pleasant and exacting to a point proper to a woman-with-yacht. The picture had grown of a second Marcia Lukas, who had been a friend of her mother's: a plumply tall woman with a leaning toward foulards and short velvet trains in the evening.

She looked at her wrist watch, and it said nine o'clock. This meant nothing so far as the passage of time was concerned, as she hadn't looked at it before. Miriam thought she had been sitting there for at least ten minutes, which would mean five, the way such things go.

Would a hundred and fifty a month be too much to ask? (*We will discuss the salary, Miss Lake, after we have met one another. So much depends upon that ephemeral value known as compatibility.*) Even two hundred a month, Miriam thought, would about approximate one of Ethel Lawton's poached eggs.

A record changed, and again the interval brought stillness. A door in the saloon's farther end opened, and a man came in. He smiled at her pleasantly, walked rapidly over to the machine, and turned it off. He was a nervous, medium man with graying hair and a precise mustache. Miriam's single view of his eyes had startled her. They seemed blank. He stood for a moment at the machine, and she saw them again, dark and brown but like glass. He walked over and held out his hand.

"Good of you to come, Miss Lake."

Miriam stood up and took his offered hand. The grip was strong, impersonal, and dry. She said, for lack of any lead more informative, "Good evening."

"Sit down, won't you?"

Not (Miriam decided) again.

"I am expecting—that is, I have an appointment to see Mrs. Murcheson."

"That's right," the man said. "That's me."

CHAPTER 3

The first impact was one of humor.

Miriam said pleasantly, "I'm afraid I don't see the point."

"This is not a joke, Miss Lake. I am Donald Murcheson. There is no Mrs. Murcheson." He smiled faintly and added, "Except in your own mind, Miriam."

Miriam thought: I'd better get out of this. He's calling me Miriam. Is this a second Floyd? It's stupid to feel like a trapped white slave. Do they still ship them to South America, or has this recent mutual hugging of friendly hemisphere-relationship stopped all that?

"I don't know what this is all about, Mr. Murcheson."

"Why not start calling me Donald? You always used to, you know. Generally with adjectives of the more invective sort."

Anger flared.

"I certainly shan't, and I didn't." (Miriam's irrepressible mind insisted: This is fishwife stuff.) "I want to be put ashore, please."

"I do wish you'd sit down, Miriam. I've had a tiring day."

"Good-by, Mr. Murcheson."

She left him smiling strangely as she hurried to the door and went out on deck. Murcheson made no attempt to follow her, to stop her, and Miriam saw with relief the dark hulk standing at the rail.

"Mr. Stone, will you please see that I'm put ashore?"

"Let me suggest a walk on deck instead. Shall we?"

"No, Mr. Stone, we will not." (Fog, yes, but through it things were drifting, as Miriam had subconsciously felt they would be drifting if the stereotyped pattern of this rankly melodramatic situation were to continue true to form.) "We're moving."

"Yes. That thing above you is the Brooklyn Bridge. Why on earth don't you get your own slicker? You have a complete outfit down in your cabin. I can't be lending you mine indefinitely."

"Mr. Stone, this possibly strikes you as amusing. It doesn't me. I've just learned that there is no Mrs. Murcheson. Undoubtedly there is also no backward little brat in need of the proper compatibility, although I've had three letters—I'm sorry if I seem to be growing incoherent, but I've had some rather beastly experiences this afternoon and evening and" (the thought struck Miriam suddenly) "I'm frightened."

"Yes. Yes, of course."

"And stop soothing me. I'm not an imbecile."

"Of course you're not."

"Don't be so hearty about it. If I were of the faintest conceivable financial value I'd feel I was being kidnapped. But I'm not. I'm not important and I'm not worth a cent. There isn't a person living who would give two cents to ransom me. Floyd certainly wouldn't. He would be astringently amused. I doubt whether there's a person living who either knows or cares whether I am here."

"Who is that Floyd?"

"That Floyd is a literary critic with a moderately adderish tongue and an aptitude for blondes."

"I don't think I'd like him. Do you?"

"No. But my emotional regard for Floyd is neither here nor there. I still consider that this is some sort of an elaborate practical joke. A very bad one. Where are we heading for?'

"The Caribbean, naturally."

Miriam stared at him in shocked astonishment.

"What?"

"Palm Cay. Where else?"

Stone's lapels were damp from fog as Miriam clutched them. She said fiercely, "I shall not have hysterics. I don't believe in them."

"That's good. It's something, anyhow."

She said more fiercely still, "Why am I wanted aboard this boat? What's the purpose?"

Stone stood there stolidly, making no protective movement to stop her shaking of him, while water hissed past in the darkness and the yacht's siren suddenly pierced fog with its shattering roar. Another blast answered from near by.

"Better come inside. That thing will blast off again at any minute." Stone added almost pleadingly, "Please come in, Miss Lake."

He did not bar her from going to the rail and leaning on it, but he did move close to her and stood tensely waiting while she looked back at the shrouded dimness of the vanishing city and then looked downward for a long time at the dark, indifferent water. He found again that this proximity to Miriam was irritatingly upsetting. It disturbed the balance of that analytical poise which Stone considered so essential to his proper study of her.

"Mr. Stone."

"Yes, Miss Lake?"

"Who are you?"

"I am Dr. Crowninshield's assistant. I hope some day to be where he is."

"And where is that?"

"At the top of his line. Even Vienna never produced anyone finer."

Doctor. (Miriam was feeling lightheaded again.) Either a Barrymore or a Lugosi. With herself the beautiful guinea pig, with her heart-shaped face and its elegant bone structure and kissable lips. Desirable. Had she missed any of the moth-eaten clichés? Pointed breasts. Some day, some-how, she hoped to run across a heroine with blunt ones. So that was it. She was to end up being toasted under a fantastic steel contraption and be turned for the sake of science into the Eternal Woman or a feminine zombie. Naturally with the transplanted brain of a criminally inclined gorilla.

"Look here, Mr. Stone, my mind is wandering but—"

"No, it isn't," he said sharply. "Don't ever, *ever* think that."

"All right. Don't get violent. But just for the sake of the record I want you to know this. My name is Miriam Lake. I'm the last specimen of a nice old family that quietly went to seed on Murray Hill and were plowed under back in twenty-nine. I've modeled for the Powers agency but never got beyond being a member of the intelligently amazed group used as a background for a new car. My social luster had dimmed to a shade where I never rated a place in the driver's seat."

"Miss Lake—"

"My stabs at being a career woman died at the receptionist's desk of a fashion magazine. A theatrical agent listened to my lyrical soprano and told me through his cigar that the gams were okay but what my delivery needed was some of those things which strippers refer to professionally as the bumps. He kindly pointed out that the customers were supposed to be rolled in the aisles and not laid out in them dead."

"Listen, Miss Lake—"

"No, you listen. Until it went up in flames this evening, I lived in a small cottage among a nest of happy Italians up in Westchester because the rent was cheap. It should have been. There, in simple fashion, I did my own chores and attempted to keep my remnant possessions from vanishing like the snowdrifts. A complete outfit of my thin wardrobe was stolen only last week."

"That—"

"*That* reduced me to the hallroom state of a man with two pairs of trousers. The recent flames cut them down to one. I owned a dear, sweet old flivver with quinsy in which I rattled daily into town trying to scare up a job. That flivver is now the proud possession of Harry in his parking lot, where it will cough itself to death. Naturally, as I am either to become a white slave or a modern version of Rider Haggard's *She*, such things are of no further concern, but they still are the simple facts. I want you to put them in a bottle and drop it overboard right after I meet my fate. It will take the place of a 'Here Lies.'"

"I must insist that you come in."

"Have you been listening to a word I've said?"

"Yes. Every word. It's quite all right. Really it is. But it's cold out here. It's wet. I cannot be responsible for your catching a chill."

"A remark," Miriam said, "that should plunge me into maniacal laughter"

As Stone opened the door, light showed her the thin, grim line of his lips and the curious watchfulness of his dark, grave eyes. It occurred to Miriam how strongly he was built and (again) what worlds of difference there were between this man and Floyd, who became through the contrast almost unpleasantly precious.

Her fright had lessened, even though Miriam realized it was only being held in abeyance until the numbness of shock would wear off. You did not feel the pain until some time had elapsed after the sock on the jaw. She forced herself to believe that no one could fear anyone so rational, so humanly solid as Stone.

Murcheson stood up and came over to greet her as she stepped into the saloon. He left a group composed of a woman, a blond young man who looked as though he would be amusing, and a thin old gentleman with a beautiful white beard. It seemed to Miriam from a distance like a kind beard, of the very best silk.

Murcheson sought and captured her hand.

"Miriam, dear, it has been several years since you've seen Aunt Kate."

"It certainly," Miriam said grimly, "has."

"Please, Miriam, *do* try not to be difficult. Kate always stood up for you. Surely you must appreciate that."

The woman was eyeing her with the liveliest interest and with a set, welcoming smile. She carried Miriam back to how things must have been when chaperons were in flower and the walls of ballrooms were edged with the glitter of important bosoms. Her features were handsomely bold, almost Roman, and were at variance with the hesitancy with which she came forward and stood for a moment quietly observing Miriam. Then she kissed Miriam and said, "Don't—please don't look at me like that. I'm your aunt Kate, dear."

It was nightmare.

Miriam drew back and said, "I doubt whether I can convince even you of this. Apparently you are determined to recognize me. I no longer feel that this situation is a joke. It has gone beyond that. There is some unfortunate, some terrible mistake. I have no Aunt Kate."

The woman seemed affronted but managed to throw a helplessly appealing glance to Murcheson and then to set her smile again.

She said, "Surely you must know that this is your cousin Forsythe, dear? My son, Forsythe Vanesse? Does nothing come back to you of those younger days? That April?"

The blond young man held out his hand with a friendliness in his smile that caused Miriam automatically to hold out her own. His features were not so bold, not so pronounced as his mother's. In fact they were infernally handsome. Which he very well knew. Miriam thought he would fit very easily into the coterie of young men who had modeled with her for Powers. Skipping, whitely toothed, along a beach in abbreviated trunks and the figure of a very flat wasp.

He repeated, "That April!" and kissed her too.

The kiss (it was a sound one) was too much. A biting, helpless sense of rage swept through Miriam. She felt on the verge of some violent, drastic action when the quiet voice of the old gentleman with the white beard stopped her. He had not risen when she came in but had sat motionless in his chair while he regarded her steadily through a thin-lensed pince-nez.

He said, "Mr. Murcheson, I must advise that we proceed more at leisure. There is danger in speed, in too rapid an accumulation of what undoubtedly are subconscious shocks. I suggest that you leave Miss Lake with me. I think it highly essential that I confer with her alone. Immediately."

CHAPTER 4

Dr. Crowninshield waited until the others had left the saloon. He smiled apologetically at Miriam and said. "You will forgive me for not having risen. You will forgive me now. My knees. Please sit down."

Pleasantness and authority were both in his voice. It enameled his air of faint humility and the disarming sweetness of the silky white beard. It bridged, Miriam thought, the Park Avenue practitioner and the autocracy of the savant from Vienna, Whatever he believed, whoever he thought her to be, he himself was thoroughly genuine.

"This is a relief, Doctor. The past half-hour has had me doubting my sanity. If someone had hailed me as Ophelia, I literally would have started strewing rosemary and myrrh, or whatever the things were in her bouquet."

"An interesting study, Ophelia. Overdrawn, perhaps, but the Elizabethan audience demanded whole tones. Ibsen was luckier. People were more prepared to accept emotional pastels. Do you miss California?"

"Miss it? I've never been there."

"I see. May I offer you a cigarette?"

"Thank you, Doctor.' She accepted the cigarette and a light. "Why did you ask me about California?"

"Do you recall ever having gone fishing, Miss Lake?"

"Yes. Frequently."

(They seemed infinitely remote, those summers at Essex, on Lake Champlain, with her mother and father; the happy, lazy afternoons on sun-sparkling waters.)

Crowninshield was saying, "Then you are familiar with worms."

"As impartially as I can be."

"I know. There is a distaste about them, but they will serve as an earthy illustration of the thought I am attempting to convey. What happens when you separate a worm into two parts?"

"Really, Doctor! I suppose you would list it as a major if highly unpleasant operation."

"It is this. Whereas to begin with you had one entity, now you have two, each independent of the other, each capable of functioning, of going about its personal business and affairs—you smile, you shudder at the thought of a worm having those things. And all this is true for a little while. At least we must pretend it is so for the purposes of our illustration. But the time comes when the worm must be joined into one entity again, otherwise the two separate individualities will sicken." He waved a beautifully modeled hand in the air. "They will die. The human mind, Miss Lake, can be like that worm."

"Just what are you driving at, Doctor?"

"I am seeking to show you that a mind, a brain, a personality—call it what you will—can be split into two parts and that each part will function as an individual entity just as you must picture the separated sections of that single worm. One half of this split brain functions, lives, has its entire being as a definite person. It is utterly distinct from, utterly unaware even of the entirely different person governed by the brain's other half. The tragedy lies, of course, in both of these separate entities being confined in the same body."

"The worms have it easier."

He refused to be amused.

"Yes, Miss Lake. Far easier."

"But that condition is schizophrenia, isn't it?"

"I have gone beyond a simple dual personality in my research. I am an adherent of the split one. Utterly and completely split. Two people living within the single body's confines and facing each other through impenetrable masks."

"Why are you telling me these things?"

"I am a believer in the therapeutic value of a clear understanding. I maintain that the rarest intelligences are frequently to be found among the insane. That, you must understand, is strictly to be regarded within certain bounds. Naturally when it comes to the manic-depressive, the senile, or general paresis—"

Crowninshield shrugged and threw Miriam a glance that insisted upon a chord of sympathetic understanding between him and herself. Her skin felt extraordinarily cold, and she knew that her face had grown clammily pale.

"Doctor, are you suggesting—are you telling me, rather, that you consider *me* insane?"

"Yes. You are the type with whom I feel I can be absolutely frank. It is a point on which my assistant, Dr. Stone, disagrees. He is young. Eliminate that horror which is making you ashen, Miss Lake. Insanity is a commonplace rather than the reverse. It is a rare man who is not touched with it. I am being brutally direct because I want you to believe in me. To trust me. Otherwise I shall not be able to help you."

"Doctor, you have never seen me before these past few minutes and yet you have the temerity, the audacity to submit a diagnosis on a stranger. I accept you as a man of standing in your profession and I insist on your accepting me as a rational human being."

"You forget, Miss Lake, that I am in detailed possession of your case history. I know everything about you. Even during these few minutes which we have passed together I feel a strong confirmation of your case history's outline. I am convinced that you are genuinely unaware of your other self."

"What other self?"

"Jennifer Murcheson. It shall be my interesting problem to restore you to it."

Miriam saw the alertly intelligent, happily engrossed look settle in Crowninshield's intensive eyes. The satisfied look of a spectator as the curtain rises upon the first act of an absorbing play. She thought: Eyes can be girded as well as loins, and he certainly is girding his.

The bland invincibility of the fetters settling about her was obvious: The more convincingly she denied that she was anyone other than Miriam Lake, the more happily eager this sweetly bearded and bright old goat would be to transform her back again into Jennifer Murcheson.

Only why? Why her? Why all of this ultra-elaborate stage setting just for her?

"Doctor, I think that I can, I *must* convince you that this is a mistake of some nature in which I have become innocently involved. I am not a celebrity. I am one of the most unimportant and valueless persons in the world. I am worth nothing except to myself. I want to live. I want, if possible, to make something out of my life. I should like to marry and establish a home. I would be happy to have a husband and children and a home's security."

"But why else am I here?"

No stranger than the other strangenesses was the momentary shock of thinking that this was not a *non sequitur* but a proposal of marriage.

"I beg your pardon?"

"I am here to give you those things. To make them possible to you again. To see to it that you once more accept your proper position in society."

"Dr. Crowninshield, it is you who must answer me. When did I leave this—my proper position in society?"

"Approximately a year ago. It has taken that long to trace you."

"Where was I a year ago?"

"You were safely at home on your ranch in southern California."

"And how long had I been there?"

"All of your life, Miss Lake."

"This is important, Doctor. I was living there two years ago? And a year and a half ago?"

"You were."

"Then if I could convince you that I had not been, would you accept the fact that this is some fantastic sort of a hoax?"

"Certainly."

"Two years ago, Doctor, I was working for the Powers agency in New York City as a model. I did that for five months. A month after that ended—which would be a year and a half ago—I started work as a receptionist in the New York office of the *Bazaar*, a fashion magazine. Will the identification and the word of responsible people in those offices convince you?"

"I fail to recall that you gave either of those places as references when you applied for the—position?"

"I felt that references of a model and an unsuccessful career woman would have no value for the post of governess to a backward child. I gave instead a general outline of my early social and intellectual background. Again, Doctor, will confirmation from the Powers agency and the *Bazaar* convince you?"

Crowninshield did not abate his lively study of her. "They would convince me completely."

"Then let us—"

"Miss Lake, the adroitness of your mind is fascinating to me. Naturally we cannot go to either of the offices you so opportunely conjure up. We are at sea."

"Because I have been trapped into coming on board. Because I am here against my will."

Crowninshield said with a certain impatience, "Surely you must find it preferable to a sanitarium? That would have had to be the alternative, you know. You must appreciate that my presence on board and that of my assistant, Dr. Stone, is not without considerable expense on the part of Mr. Murcheson. Would he have gone to this bother, this expenditure, if you were what you claim? A stranger? A nobody? Are you seriously asking me to believe that such a thing could be so?"

"It is so, Doctor."

"Have you received any treatment other than the greatest courtesy? I assure you that everything has been arranged for your peace of mind and comfort. Your movements will be to all purposes free of any restraint. Every effort will be exerted to meet your wishes."

"May I send radiograms?"

"I have no doubt but that you may send as many as you wish."

"Then would radio confirmation from the Powers agency and the *Bazaar* help to convince you?"

Crowninshield looked at her for the first time with a trace of puzzled speculation.

"They would have a certain tendency to, Miss Lake." Miriam stood up.

"Will you come with me? Will you come with me right now to the wireless room?"

Crowninshield laboriously (his knees) got to his feet. He crossed to a panel and pressed a button.

He said, "Fascinating!"

"What is?"

"'You are perfectly aware that this is Saturday night, that the business offices are closed. You are aware that no replies could be received earlier than, say, around noon on Monday." He came close to her and said with patient kindness, "Do not let this other self of yours, this present Miriam Lake, fight so hard. Naturally she is contesting every step of the way. She is fighting for her life. I know that. Because when Jennifer Murcheson is born again Miriam Lake will die. I must beg of you to carry this thought always with you: let Jennifer Murcheson come back. There is nothing to lose and everything to gain. As Jennifer you will cease to be the penniless nobody to whom you now so desperately cling and will find that security you desire. Wealth. Great wealth."

Some curious prompting caused Miriam to ask, "Wealth—and what else, Doctor?"

He smiled patiently.

"That I do not know. I am a psychiatrist and not a fortuneteller. Shall we defer the radiograms until Monday morning?"

A steward came in, came over to them, with his eyes on Miriam in a fashion which under normal circumstances she would have labeled devouringly flattering. He struck her as a bright-faced twenty, scrubbed to the pink, with a sparkling crew cut of chestnut hair and a tailor-made uniform if ever. Not a muscle missed.

"You rang, miss?"

"Dr. Crowninshield rang."

"Will you suggest to Mrs. Vanesse that she join us, please?"

"Certainly, Doctor."

"I believe she is playing bridge in the library."

"Yes, sir."

The steward left, and Crowninshield placed a hand lightly on Miriam's shoulder.

"You are tired."

"I'm not tired. I am confused and thoroughly angry."

"Mrs. Vanesse will show you to your cabin. Let her comfort you. You will take off your hat, your jacket, your gloves. You will change into something that will bring ease." The pressure of his fingers on her shoulder strengthened. "Do not stand poised for flight. There can be no flight. You are a young woman of strong character, and as such you will accept the inevitable. We touch no port for many days."

She regarded searchingly his kind and speculative eyes, finding an immense sympathy in them in company with their strong curiosity. He withdrew his hand from her shoulder suddenly, as though he were just aware of having made the gesture and seemed abashed by it.

"I suppose there is no one on board who is not aware of my—condition? Even the officers and men of the crew?"

"No one, Miss Lake. Such general knowledge seemed essential for your safety."

"I doubt whether honest anger has ever driven anyone to suicide, Doctor."

"I am sure that it hasn't. We must except, of course, the scorpion, which is reputed at times to sting itself to death from sheer rage. But there are other considerations to hold in account. Safety, Miss Lake, can occasionally lie along many lines."

CHAPTER 5

The cabin was charming and opened into a dressing room which in turn led to a bath. The rooms were on the port side amidships, and their portholes were high enough above the water line to permit their being kept open in anything except bad weather.

Mrs. Vanesse had been scrupulously impersonal on their way below, filling the brief passage with social small talk of the most general nature. There was a disturbing terror in this to Miriam more deep than silence would have been, or open attack on the problem which was enfolding her softly, mesh by mesh, in its golden web.

Mrs. Vanesse looked out of a porthole and said, "We're leaving Ambrose Channel. The fog has lifted. Those lights over there are Coney Island. It is curious how they have always seemed more like getting home to me, when returning from abroad, than the Statue of Liberty. I have never been to Coney Island. Someday I want to go. The swell is becoming noticeable, don't you think?"

"I do, Mrs. Vanesse."

The woman turned, and there was something pathetically touching in her dominating eyes, a pathos that softened their confident look of arrogant boldness.

"Wouldn't you—couldn't you find it possible to call me Kate, dear?"

"I am sorry, but I could not. I feel the absolute futility even of speaking. I have never knowingly seen anyone on this boat before tonight."

"We understand that, Miriam. Dr. Crowninshield has explained."

"The doctor has flattered me to the extent of stating that I have a strong character. I suppose it was an oblique manner of pointing out the ultimate softening results of batting your head against a stone wall. No one can keep doing so indefinitely. I am at a loss to convince him, to convince any of you of your mistake until Monday morning."

"Monday?"

"Until the Powers and the *Bazaar* offices are open."

"Would you explain that, dear?"

Miriam did, and Mrs. Vanesse listened to her with growing concern.

She said, after Miriam had finished, "Will you promise me one thing?"

"Yes?"

"Do not let the replies you will receive bother you too greatly."

Miriam thought: Dr. Crowninshield undoubtedly believes that there will be no restriction placed upon my sending radiograms. Outwardly there may be none. There is no guarantee that they will really be sent or that any replies received will not be doctored or entirely fictitious.

Mrs. Vanesse's concern deepened.

"Let me—you must let me—I can't bear seeing you like this."

She moved quickly with the lightness and grace which is always so astonishing in many large women and took off Miriam's hat. She placed it on a dresser and said, "Your jacket, and do take off your gloves, dear. Then I want to show you something."

Miriam put her jacket on a chair and her gloves beside the hat. Fog damp had reduced its perkiness considerably. It had the aloof and sheep-ish look of a rained-on, handsome cat. The swell had increased as the yacht headed into open water, and the unaccustomed movement added to the bewildering lightness in her head.

"You will have your sea legs in no time, dear," Mrs. Vanesse said. "Once a good sailor always a good sailor. It is like bicycle-riding or the breast stroke. Come with me."

Miriam followed Mrs. Vanesse into the dressing room and watched her slide back the panels of a wardrobe. A rack of dresses, suits, and coats faced her. Below them were shoes and slippers, while above, on stands fastened to a shelf, were hats. It looked like the discriminating loot of the town's best shops.

Mrs. Vanesse said, "They will fit. If there should be any minor altera-tions required, one of the stewardesses is an excellent seamstress. She is an elderly Belgian woman and amuses herself when not on duty by making the most exquisite lace. I have bought several pieces of it and will show them to you."

"So this is why that entire outfit of mine was stolen, Mrs. Vanesse. I regret having blamed my neighbors."

"Dear—*please*, not stolen. How otherwise could we have got the proper sizes?"

"Was it also necessary to burn the house down, Mrs. Vanesse? To burn my keepsakes, the few memories I had left?"

Mrs. Vanesse drew her breath in sharply. Her face paled, accenting its rouge.

"Fire? I do not understand that—tell me!"

"When I got back there this evening from town the house had been burned to the ground. Wasn't that unnecessarily cruel? I only had a few things, but they meant a lot to me."

"No—I must insist, dear. It was an accident. We had nothing to do with it. Nothing, I tell you." Mrs. Vanesse went on hurriedly in an obvious effort to dismiss the incident completely. "Come, your other things are over here." Drawers in a wide chest offered a smart assortment of silk lingerie, stockings, and accessories. The bathroom into which Mrs. Vanesse insisted on leading Miriam was stocked with her favorite line of creams and cosmetics. The tub seemed of black onyx, and it served as a curiously inappropriate background for the impassioned quality which suddenly came into Mrs. Vanesse's voice.

"Miriam—we have been instructed to continue calling you Miriam for a while—surely, my dear, you cannot believe that Donald would have gone to this care, this loving care, if there had been any doubt? Somewhere through this dark curtain that is blinding you there must filter some memory of Donald's character? Its fineness? Its lovable selflessness?"

"I shall be sorry for his disappointment. I am almost beginning to think I shall feel sorry for myself. There is an Aladdin touch."

"Thank God—you smile."

"I believe that was also a habit with the contemporaries of Marie Antoinette."

"Marie Antoinette, dear? I don't catch the allusion?"

"The face her friends arranged to present to the guillotine."

"Don't—I beg of you not to talk like that. You will come up with me now? You will join us? We're playing bridge. You will cut in?"

"I have something to show you, Mrs. Vanesse."

Miriam went back into the cabin and opened her bag. She took the three letters from it.

She said, "Why was I tricked?"

Mrs. Vanesse glanced at the envelopes negligently and then put them down on the dresser top.

"I do not have to read them, dear. I wrote them."

"Why?"

"Because Dr. Crowninshield instructed me to."

So it was back again to White Beard. Something like playing with froth which vanished just when you felt you had captured a solid handful.

"Would you care to change? That button will summon your stewardess. She is a very capable woman called Biddle. She looks amazingly like an important rip, but so many of the most efficient stewardesses do. Or perhaps you prefer to come up just as you are?"

There were such courtesy and consideration in Mrs. Vanesse's manner that Miriam found herself almost apologetic.

"Would it offend you very much if I were to stay here?" Mrs. Vanesse gave a faint sigh of resignation.

"We generally play until around midnight. Do come up if you change your mind. We will be most happy if you do." The door closed.

CHAPTER 6

Instantly it was maddening to be alone.

Frequently Miriam had spent a whole series of lonely evenings in the cottage up in Westchester, but there had been nothing to restrict her to that solitude other than her own determination. There had been rare exceptions when she had run into town and joined Floyd in the minor *divertissements* at which he had seen fit to parade her, but otherwise her existence had slowly been drifting toward that of a hermit.

It had never occurred to Miriam to ask herself the reason for this, and when she had considered the matter at all she had set it down vaguely to the out-of-the-way location of the cottage. It never struck her for a minute that she herself could do with some emotional readjustment. Nor did it occur to her to wonder why with the average talents which she possessed in addition to her undeniably attractive looks she had not succeeded in retaining an average job.

As for any contact with her childhood milieu, that was completely gone, and she had never seriously questioned herself as to just why. Chance, she felt, had separated her during the past decade completely from her friends of years back, and even then there had never been many.

Nona Stevenson had married a commander in the navy, and her last Christmas card had come from a China station. The Olcott girls had also been caught in the financial debacle, their father had "accidentally" fallen from an office window in a twentieth floor on Wall Street, and they had gone abroad to eke out their scant means. Heaven knew where they were now. One or two others. That elderly friend of her parents, Ida Mayford, whom Miriam had called on perhaps twice during the past good many years.

Ida Mayford: a frail shell in lavenders with a dried-apricot face and a mind that had been wandering backward toward childhood. She still lived (if she were alive at all) in the Mayford brownstone front on Madison Avenue where she had indulged in a perverted delight in hiring and firing entire batches of servants. Ida had once explained to Miriam that it was the only form of exercise she any longer permitted herself.

Miriam could imagine the reception which Mrs. Mayford would give to a perfectly literal radiogram stating: "Have been shanghaied aboard

Murcheson yacht. Notify coast guard effect my release. Heading south for Palm Cay in Caribbean." Mrs. Mayford's reply, if she bothered to reply, would undoubtedly follow her usual peculiar vagaries and say: "So glad for you, dear. Best love. Ida."

What about Floyd? Just what about him? He would be either sore at her having clung to the Victorian modesties or else blind drunk, or in the arms of the Venus who had them. He would take the wire as a gag. Either as a gag or her very just deserts. No, not that; but he would never take it seriously.

Ida was the best bet in spite of her vaguenesses. Certainly it was worth a chance. Miriam went into the dressing room and opened the wardrobe. She put on a moleskin jacket and left the cabin.

The passageway was empty and she met no one on her way upstairs and out onto the deck. As Mrs. Vanesse had announced, the fog had lifted entirely. There was no moon, but the cloudless black purple of the night was pierced with stars. Water hissed with the rip of silk and a breeze sang thinly in the rigging.

Miriam took it for granted that the wireless room would be on the bridge deck somewhere near the charthouse. She mounted a ladder onto the darkness of the bridge. Through a window a gleam glowed from the binnacle, making faintly visible the bulking form of a quartermaster at the wheel. Then a man was beside her, quietly, suddenly, dimly featured beneath the visor of an officer's cap.

"Miss Lake? I am the first mate. Jack Richardson."

"I am looking for the wireless room, Mr. Richardson."

"Let me show you. It's along here."

"Thank you."

"It cleared up splendidly, didn't it?"

"Didn't it."

"We'll probably run into weather off Hatteras, but it may not be much. The glass is dropping a little. I hope we get the breaks down below. The hurricane season is due to start. Nasty animals, hurricanes. Ever been through one?"

"Never."

"They give you a turn. I don't care how seasoned you are. Allow me—there's a little movement up here, more so than below."

Richardson steadied her with a hand carefully cupped about an elbow.

"I am not accustomed to anything more unstable than the temperamental leaps of my flivver."

Richardson decided that this was tremendously funny. He laughed at some length. He said, "That's a *good* one." He opened a door into a businesslike-looking room neatly spaced with apparatus.

"Sparks, Miss Lake wants to send a message. This is Jerry Simmonds."

"How do you do, Miss Lake?"

"Mr. Simmonds."

She thought him a depressed youngster. Weedy, and dour long before his years, with a brooding eye that looked straight through her and out into interstellar space. Lida Wilbury's boy had been like that; always knotted on a couch with some esoteric magazine on the fantasies of science. Simmonds' fingers were long and scandalously black over an underlay of nicotine.

Richardson left them, and Simmonds placed a second chair at the desk and produced message blanks and a perfectly sharpened pencil. Miriam faced the blank. She wrote: "Mrs. Tomlinson Mayford," and then the address on Madison Avenue, New York. She wrote nothing else but sat considering the blank for a long time. Simmonds, equally motionless, went on with his brooding.

Time lengthened.

The wind in the rigging sang the only sound.

"What is the name of this yacht, Mr. Simmonds?"

"The *Donna Louise*."

"Two words?"

"Yes." He spelled them out. "It's a funny name for a boat. It's funny for anything. Louise isn't Spanish that I know of. Do you?"

"No."

"Could be an American wife of a Spanish don, of course."

"It could."

"People go straight off the beam when they name boats. It's the same way with Pullman cars. I hit New York from New Orleans on the *Tulip*. Nothing could have been more incongruous, do you think?"

"Nothing."

With an utter disregard for consequences, brought on by a surge of swift anger, Miriam wrote: "Am aboard the Murcheson yacht *Donna Louise* heading for Palm Cay in Caribbean. Shanghaied by employment ruse. Notify coast guard effect my release."

The pencil trailed, and she shrugged hopelessly. She pushed the blank over toward Simmonds.

"You would never send anything like that, would you?"

He read the message impassively.

"I can get a ruling on it if you wish, but I'm afraid it would be an awful waste of time."

"I feel that, too."

Miriam tore the message blank up slowly.

"I'm sorry, Miss Lake, but my orders are to have all of your messages checked by the owner." A half smile brought strangely pleasant lights to his dour face. He said earnestly, "It is for your own good."

She made no effort to move, and Simmonds selected several of the message scraps and formed them into cornucopias. Crowninshield had been partly wrong. She could send messages if she wanted to, but they would first have to be censored by Donald Murcheson.

For what dark purpose?

The phrase took root. It became an assurance of some evil design the flowering of which was in no way plain. In paradox, her worthlessness seemed to be of inestimable worth to one or more of the people on board. It must be so in order to justify this great elaboration.

Miriam stood up.

"You have your work to do."

"There is nothing until the news comes through at eleven. It is only ten after ten now."

"Good night. And thank you anyhow, Mr. Simmonds."

"It's all right, Miss Lake."

He remained seated and added a delicately completed cornucopia to the pile. Miriam left the room and caught a view again of Simmonds as she passed an open port. She paused to watch him gather up the fragments of her message.

He put them in an envelope.

He put the envelope in a drawer.

CHAPTER 7

Miriam stood still in the darkness and considered what this meant, this careful hoarding of the scraps of her message to Ida. Would they be given to Murcheson for his sardonic inspection, or would they be given to Crowninshield to mull over and to measure beneath the yardstick of psychiatry? She regretted not having gathered them up herself and having thrown them into the sea.

Richardson was waiting near the ladder. His face, in the night's pale darkness, was eagerly friendly. It fitted in with the whole keynote of this general friendliness which was becoming for Miriam so increasingly terrifying. A good, honest out-and-out menace or villain would almost have been a relief. Less of this beamishness and a little more Simon Legree. "Did you talk with Simmonds at all, Miss Lake?"

"We chatted a little. About Pullman cars."

"Really? He's a curious chap. Very brilliant in his way. He knits."

"Socks?"

"Socks, mufflers—anything. Says he's going in for petit point if he ever gets around to it."

"It is the sort of thing you have to creep up on."

"I dare say. Did you get the messages off all right?" Miriam did not answer directly, but smiled at Richardson and wished him good night. She left him standing at the ladder head. The main deck was empty and cheerlessly bleak under a faint light that bathed it through the ports. This emptiness, this bleakness drove her swiftly into a chill of fear. Her nerves responded as so many willing chords to the tune of the heard but unseen terror of the sea, which had suddenly become inimical to her, its rugged friendliness gone.

She stopped at a porthole. Inside there were lights and warmth and the beautiful room. Background music of a placid charm came from the Empire case. Crowninshield was sitting across a bridge table from Forsythe Vanesse, while Murcheson faced Mrs. Vanesse. Stone, at length in a deep armchair, was reading a book.

Miriam stood clinging to this picture of peaceful domesticity and thought of herself as of all the waifs in peril who pressed their noses against lighted windowpanes at Christmastides from their stance in the snow outside. A welter of self-pity swamped her, bringing her to the verge of tears. Give me (she thought) a package of matches and a cathedral steps and I'm set.

She was conscious through the faint mist in her eyes that Stone had stopped reading and was looking at her. He gave no sign to the others that she was there but stood up and walked rapidly toward the door.

He said as he joined her on the darkened deck, "Thank heaven that at last you have put on a proper coat."

He no longer regarded her as a fragile egg but took her arm in his and led her to the afterdeck and to a comfortable settee in the shelter of the deck housing.

"You mustn't mind me if you want to cry. Go right ahead. Just think of me as not being here."

"I do not want to cry."

"Then there certainly is a leak in your eye mechanism."

"Dr. Stone, I had hoped to send a message to a friend. I realized it was hopeless. What I would want to say would be prohibited for my own good. I could not resist looking in. I have never felt so miserable, so lonely, or so frightened in my life."

Curious, this warmth. This heady desire which Stone felt sweeping over him to comfort, shelter, and protect. He examined it suspiciously and labeled it properly for what it was: the biological urge in its most sinister manifestations. He had felt strong quivers of it long ago with Elsa Davis, but they, fortunately, had impelled him into nothing more drastic than that pink valentine. This was different. And it wasn't a quiver. Firmly, quickly, it would have to be suppressed. If it were not, she'd be making a fool out of him, too.

He said, "All that will pass, Miss Lake. A good night's sleep will bring better adjustment."

"I have a feeling that I can trust you. That I can also trust Dr. Crowninshield. I would be as insane as he believes me to be if I felt that I could trust anyone else. Both of you are dupes, as I am a dupe. Only I know it. You don't." Stone stretched his head back and looked up at stars. Her voice was touchingly musical, pitched right, a little on the low. Not any night-club deathbed soprano gurgling out last gasps for her man, rather a well-cast bell. He had a feeling for voices. They meant more to him than almost anything else about a person.

"You are being very foolish to battle against all of this," he said. "Luxury and security in a world where there is little enough of either left." He turned his head and looked directly at her, then thought better of it and turned it swiftly away again. "Your cousin Forsythe seems a very decent fellow."

"He is not my cousin, but I have no doubt he is a very decent fellow. He is certainly an ornamental one. He would grace any lido with the greatest of ease."

"What does April mean to you?"

"April, Dr. Stone, means exactly April."

"An April of about six years ago when you were sixteen?"

"Any April around six years ago would have found me fourteen, a worldly-wise student at Miss Davidge's school for the female young where the remnant dregs of the family wealth were spent to keep me. The dregs held out one year. My father held out for two. My mother was already dead. I loved them both. Put away your Aprils, Dr. Stone. I'm going to bed."

He was back again instantly in his professional shell.

"If Dr. Crowninshield were to fix a mild sedative, would you take it?"

"No."

"He was afraid that you would not. I just thought I'd ask."

Stone accompanied her to the deck below and along the passageway to her cabin. He hesitated at the door, finding it difficult to wish her good night. It was an inadequate phrase for expressing the confusions she roused in him: an earnest wish for her well-being and a bitter distaste in his private opinion concerning this unkind thing which he felt her to be doing.

Fear was there, too. A dread that Crowninshield might be absolutely right and he, Stone, wrong. This opened a road toward peril which he did not wish her to travel along alone, without the most expert help. She was very beautiful. A beauty with a strange sadness veining it. He would have liked to tell her everything he thought. He did not dare.

He said with a dark earnestness, "We are here if you feel that you need us. All of us are ready at any moment to help you. No matter at what hour of the night."

CHAPTER 8

The woman's hair was dyed a vivid shade of henna, and little lines graven in her face were suggestive of drink. They were the result of endless shore leaves along the world's water fronts spent in maritime bars hoisting slugs of straight rye. She had a tall, skinny look but wore her stewardess's uniform with an air. A bracelet of butterfly wings pressed in glass glowed with emerald drops about a thin wrist.

"I'm Biddle, Miss Lake. Give me your coat and I'll hang it up."

"Thank you."

"What do you use, a nightgown or pajamas?"

"A nightgown, please."

"I like them better, too. It's smooth tonight, isn't it?"

"I am getting more used to the motion."

"How do you like your bath? Real hot or just moderate?"

"Just moderate."

"This certainly is a honey." Biddle placed a sheer nightgown of pale peach on the turned-down bed. "I blew myself to one something like it once in Yokohama. Have you ever been to Yokohama?"

"No."

"It's nothing much. I stayed at the New Grand on Yamashitacho and took in the earthquake museum and some of the temples and drank a lot of rye. I leave it alone except when I'm on shore, so don't worry about that. Murray is bringing you some sandwiches and milk. He's the room and deck steward. Would you rather have the milk warmed, or would you rather have champagne? Mrs. Vanesse always has a pint of champagne with her night lunch. She says the milk curdles in her stomach and makes her dream."

"I'll have the milk. I really want nothing."

"Well, it will be here anyhow in case you change your mind. Is there anything else I can do for you?"

"Nothing, Biddle. And thank you."

Biddle opened the door. She hesitated for an instant and then said, "Just push that button if you want me." The little lines seemed to deepen, to tighten sharply in her face. "If you want me for anything at all, Miss Lake."

"Thank you, and good night."

Biddle looked down the passageway.

"Here's Murray now."

Biddle left, and the young steward with the crew haircut took her place. He smiled and came in and placed a silver tray on a table. There were sandwiches, a glass, a small pitcher of milk.

"Will this be all right?"

"Thank you, Murray."

"Sure you don't want anything else?"

"No, nothing."

This was not true, because Miriam would have liked him to stay, with his scrubbed face and eager young smile and the muscles rippling so serviceably beneath the tailored cloth. She would have liked Biddle to stay, too, with her friendly matter-of-fact chatter. She smiled back at Murray and, after he had gone, stood looking at the closed door. She turned its bolt and started to undress.

It was novel to lie in scented warmness while watching the water in the tub swing lazily with the motion of the ship. It brought a fatalistic and hypnotizing sense of comfort, and Miriam realized that she was incredibly tired.

It seemed curious how this moment fulfilled the general ultimate of her desires: privacy, solid comfort, no pressure of business or of household cares, a good bed, a good book. There had been several books on the bed table. One, the diary of a foreign press correspondent, she had been wanting to read for weeks. Floyd had said he would get her a copy of it but he never had.

How different Floyd's life and milieu were from a man like Stone's. Worlds apart. One a closed room heavy with cocktail odors and expensive scent, bitter brittle talk underlain with fear, with the fear at anything so suicidal as being banal, the other the fields and sea and wind. Possibly she was romanticizing in that, but she did not think so. Stone was very real.

She got ready for bed.

Miriam stood for a while and considered the sandwiches and milk. She separated thin slices of bread and found authentic *foie gras*. Ages had passed since she had had any of it. Caviar, too, between thin buttered rye. She took the plate and a glass of milk and put them on the bed table beside the books. She thought it stupid even to consider the possibility of their being drugged. Such gestures were blatant with crudity, and nothing so far had been crudely done.

Miriam turned out all lights but a bed lamp. She thought she would leave it burning all night. The diary was engrossing from the start.

An hour passed measurelessly.

Toward midnight she heard the faint rapping on the door.

It shocked her into a nervous tremor. She threw on a bathrobe and slid into mules. She went over to the door.

"Yes? Who is it?"

There was no reply, but the white square of a folded sheet of paper suddenly showed on the floor at her feet. She stooped down and picked it up.

I believe in you (the note read) *and will help you if I can. Your situation is of the most dangerous nature. Murder is its root. I beg of you to be constantly on your guard and not to be driven to any irremediable extreme. I beg of you, too, to destroy this at once. If you do not, and were this writing to be traced, I would pay the forfeit with my life.*

Miriam's instant shaken thought was that the sender of the note was Stone. She did not stop to rationalize this, but mingled with her own sharp sense of fear was an urgent wish to shelter him from this gesture which, according to the note itself, was all but quixotically suicidal. There was an ash tray on the bed table and a folder of matches. The note writhed in glowing curls.

She crushed it into ash.

CHAPTER 9

Miriam disliked futile gestures and, considering the moment it had taken to burn the note, she felt it would be useless to open the cabin door on the chance that Stone would still be there. It remained fixed in her mind that it was he who had sent it, possibly because she wished it so. It did not (right then) occur to her to doubt the contradictions in the anonymity of the note and its melodramatically grim import with the forthrightness in Stone's character as she herself had conceived it.

She unbolted and opened the door.

A stewardess was walking along the passageway. It was not Biddle, her chatty one. This was a wiry, tall woman with gray hair drawn slickly back over her skull and ending in an impressive bun at the nape of her neck. She examined Miriam calmly through steel-rimmed spectacles.

She said with a touch of foreign accent, "Is there something I can do for you, Miss Lake?"

"Come in, will you?"

"Certainly." The woman came in and said, "I am Leclos. I take care of Mrs. Vanesse."

"You are the Belgian woman? The one who makes lace?"

"Yes. You are trembling. Have you a chill?"

"I think I have."

"With your permission?"

Leclos went into the dressing room and returned with a woolen wrapper.

"This will be warmer, Miss Lake."

"Thank you."

"Shall I call Dr. Crowninshield?"

"No. I think just my nerves. It will pass."

"You would wish me to stay with you for a little while? Or would you prefer Biddle?"

Miriam thought: She does not suggest calling Mrs. Vanesse.

"I think I am all right now. I wonder—was there anyone in the passageway? Other than yourself?"

"No. Did something disturb you?"

"It seemed to me that someone stumbled."

Leclos smiled thinly.

"The passageway is carpeted. The door is well constructed. You would hear no one walking, even stumbling, Miss Lake." Leclos did not alter the dispassionate steadiness of her regard. "A ship at sea creates its own diverse noises. I am afraid that we are in for weather by the time we shall find ourselves off Hatteras."

"Thank you for coming in. Good night."

Leclos made no movement toward the door.

"I think that you are eager to talk, Miss Lake. There are moments when even the commonplaces of the most banal sort of causerie are soothing."

"Then will you sit down?"

"Thank you. If you wish."

"You must know the nature of my coming on board?"

"All of us have been instructed."

"I am tired of this crying out into the wilderness, of stating myself to be myself. How long have you been in service?"

"I signed on for the southern cruise last fall. We called at all of the principal ports of the eastern coast of South America. Mr. Murcheson was engaged in some social research. The boat has been in commission ever since."

"You will have formed some judgment of Mr. Murcheson?"

"Naturally. Everyone relaxes when at sea. They become more genuine, more of their true selves. It is curiously like the masquerade balls that were so popular in my youth. It is the sea itself which offers a mask, the isolation from the routine of life ashore which serves as a domino. These truer selves can be for the better or for the worse."

"And Mr. Murcheson?"

"Mr. Murcheson is a charitable and a very honorable man. He is a true philanthropist because his good deeds are never publicized or bruited around." Leclos added with delicate emphasis: "Everyone in his employ is devoted to him. Almost, Miss Lake, to the point of blindness."

"Were Mrs. Vanesse and her son also on board last winter?"

"No, this is their first sailing with the *Donna Louise* that I know of. They have lived largely abroad and were in France until conditions there grew so impossible that they decided to return."

"But you have formed some opinion of them?"

"I shall be frank because we have been instructed to show the utmost consideration to your wishes, even to a whim. Ordinarily I would consider such discussion an impropriety. You will understand that, Miss Lake?"

"Perfectly."

"Then I would say that Mrs. Vanesse is a woman burdened with a terrible problem upon her heart. One believes this from several minute things, from a prolonged vagueness in the eyes followed by a sharp concentration when the beclouding thought has crystallized into a point so penetrative that it stabs. Throughout my life I have found such moments of abstraction to be of a significance the most profound. Above all I consider Mrs. Vanesse a gracious lady."

"And her son?"

"Mr. Forsythe Vanesse is possessed of that wit and that facile charm only natural to such a birth and the cosmopolitan background of his upbringing." Leclos studied her placid hands through the steel-rimmed spectacles. "It is difficult to find the precise niche for such a one. He has many faces. Each has the facet of a well-cut gem and is pleasant to look upon. I can offer no proper précis of young Mr. Vanesse." The words were equable enough, but the perplexity which ran strongly through them seemed in some indefinable fashion to offer a warning note in this general atmosphere of philanthropy, ladylike graciousness, and rather emphasized aura of good will.

"I think you feel more in regard to Mr. Vanesse than you care to say."

"No, I must ask you to believe me quite sincere. Where so many aspects of engaging openness exist it is impossible to recognize the real truth of the whole."

A heavier sea than any met as yet sent a shudder through the yacht, and the sound was clear of a hand slapped sharply, suddenly against the door.

A voice called in from the passageway.

"Sorry if I disturbed you. I lurched."

Leclos said quietly, "That is the voice of Mr. Vanesse."

"It's quite all right," Miriam called.

"Are you in bed?"

"Practically."

"That's an impossibility. In this sea you're either in a place or out. Want anything?"

"No, thank you."

"Good night, then."

"Good night."

Leclos stood up.

"The bridge game will have finished. I have my usual duties to perform in Madam's cabin. With your permission I will attend to them."

"Thank you again, Leclos."

"It has been of interest, Miss Lake."

Leclos left, and Miriam bolted the door. She got into bed and tried to lose herself once more in the diary of the foreign correspondent, but always between her and the printed page swam the ghost of that warning note. Sharpest among all its words stood out: "Murder is its root."

Murder of her? Of murder already done? By Donald Murcheson, by his sister, or by her son? Three people of such elegant nicenesses whose hearts were flaunted on their sleeves for the very good deed of proving her to be a young woman of great wealth. Suppose she were to yield, to pretend to remember that aureate self they were so avid to bestow upon her, what then?

Murder is its root.

A phrase came back to Miriam which she had read in some authoritative source: that the proof of a crime lay first in an ability to offer circumstantial evidence that a crime had actually been committed. This, in murder, meant the corpus delicti. This (the statement had gone on) was required in murder, except at sea.

Except at sea.

The sickening thought of this, the dread, almost made Miriam ill. A possible simplicity of plot focused with deadly sharpness: Suppose the true Jennifer Murcheson were dead? Were murdered? Suppose Miriam herself were being groomed into making an admission which would publicly endow her with Jennifer Murcheson's identity, so that once this identity were satisfactorily established, Miriam could "disappear overboard while on the high seas"? But why want to murder Jennifer Murcheson again?

It could be important that the body, the corpus delicti of the true Jennifer Murcheson, never be found. That (if this line of thought were the true explanation) the body lie concealed in its safe grave among the barren hills of southern California. For if the body *were* found, a postmortem would reveal that murder had been done. Whereas on the other hand, if Miriam (as Jennifer Murcheson) were to be lost overboard there would be no post-mortem, and "Jennifer Murcheson" would be legally listed as having suffered an accidental death. Not murder.

Which of those three?

Was Donald Murcheson the murderer, or Kate Vanesse, or Forsythe her son?

All of them? Two of them?

Why?

The gilding of large wealth covered them, and still such a murder surely would have had its origin in gain? Dimly a ship's bell was struck twice. One o'clock. There was the feeling that, very quietly, no one slept. That near her, about her, each lay awake while constructing his thought and plans upon her life. Certainly that in the brain of one of them there revolved a studious conjecturing as to the perfect moment, of how and when and where it would arrive, for her plunge into the water with its ever concealing grave.

Even Miriam's small comfort from her belief that Stone had sent the warning note began to fade. It was becoming less and less in character, less of the sort of thing which he would do. He would never be devious. But if not Stone, who was this friend? Was it a friend? Could its purpose have been the very reverse? A subtle attempt to drive her through accumulating terror into a desperation so frantic that she might even take her own life? And so save the murderer the bother of it.

Murder is its root.

Exhaustion carried the phrase into Miriam's restless sleep. A tragic chant sang ceaselessly behind closed eyes.

CHAPTER 10

Sunday was to be pointed with fragmentary episodes, each of small importance in itself, but each serving as a separate force. And the total of all these minor forces was to be summed up during the night in the common field of death.

The morning ushered in brooding weather. Sullen clouds occupied the sky over gusts of wind, while the sea had a forceful slap. Miriam felt that she had had no rest. To her gloomy thoughts the wardrobe offered a variety of shrouds. She chose a knitted dress of somber violet. She did not ring for Biddle.

All this day, this Sunday and its night stretched in front of her before Monday would come and the problematical ability to radio the Powers office and the *Bazaar* in that attempt to convince Crowninshield of her true identity. This loomed now as an attempt already doomed to failure. Miriam knew in her heart that it would be circumvented in the very nicest way.

It was eight o'clock. People on yachts never breakfasted at eight o'clock. Not in any of the yacht-inclusive movies Miriam had seen. She was hungry. It was this damned sea air. Or was it simply consistent with her fate? Prisoners under the death sentence invariably acquired a good appetite and flashed out on a stomachful of steak. Or so Miriam understood. A reversal of the Egyptian habit of leaving baked meats in the tomb. Nowadays you took them with you. She wanted to cry.

The passageway was empty. It was always empty. The sea when she reached the deck was an angered living force of sheet steel. Frothing. Little froths of madness at its mouth. Miriam clutched the guard rail and took deep breaths of chill, clean air while spray whipped past reduced to spindrift. Here was an intoxicating quality urgent for vigorous living, and Miriam would have found it deliriously exhilarating under circumstances less lethal. Because her last night's formula for the plot remained.

There was Murray, the crew-cropped young steward, as scrubbed and blithely muscled as ever. The deck could have been a calm platter for all it affected his easy gait as he gracefully met bound with bound and stopped beside Miriam with a smug look of poised ease. Almost ballet.

Murray said with all the conviction of the obvious, "Up early, Miss Lake."

"I suppose I am."

"Brisk."

"Yes, isn't it."

"Looking for breakfast?"

"Very much so."

"I'll show you to the dining saloon."

"You'll carry me to it, I'm afraid."

"Oh, you'll get used to this in no time. Just wait until tomorrow. This is nothing."

"Well, in my language it's something."

"Forget it and it won't bother you. Ignore it."

"I suppose riveters on skyscrapers use the same formula."

"Absolutely the same idea. Or when you're learning to skate. We'll go in through here."

The dining saloon was paneled in teak and hung with Gobelins. Miriam thought: It would be. And the naperies will be of the whitest and everything will be served piping hot in crested sterling-silver warmers. Murray held her chair back while she sat down at the table.

"I'll let Branch know you are here. Branch is the steward."

"Thank you."

Murray left. He was shortly replaced by Branch, a pleasingly plump man with a long nose. Branch said good morning. He asked Miriam what she would have.

"Orange juice and coffee, please."

"How would you like broiled kidneys with mushrooms?"

"I'd like them very much. I would feel stunned."

"Toast or muffins, Miss Lake? Or do you prefer popovers?"

"Certainly popovers. I haven't had them for years."

"Spinoff makes good ones. He's the chef. Used to cook for the Czar. They're not just shells all hollow in the middle."

"I am looking forward to lots of middle."

"Hot milk, with the coffee, or cream?"

"Just cream."

Branch left. Miriam reviewed her order for breakfast and thought: And *much* better than the death-house meals at Sing Sing. Then Branch was back almost immediately with a typewritten sheet.

"The morning wireless news, Miss Lake."

"Thank you."

He left and Miriam glanced at items which were rather gloomily colored, she thought, by the dour radio operator Simmonds. She recognized his touch: a certain zestful relish about the headlines that would have found high favor among ghouls.

ENTIRE RED DIVISIONS SLAUGHTERED

NAZI DEAD LIE HEAPED IN FIELDS

BOMBED HAMBURG SECTIONS SHAMBLES

TAXES TO BE TERRIFIC

ROOSEVELT DIRE

Dire what? Dire how? Miriam was pursuing this when Branch came in with orange juice. He was followed by Forsythe.

"Well," Forsythe said, "this is luck. Think of you being up. And think of me being up."

And a polished job he had made of it, Miriam decided. Accoutered to the inch. Plaid sports coat over corduroy slacks. A turkey-red scarf that matched glow for glow with his deep tan. A fine white and twinkle in his eye and a spray of ozone over the lot of it.

Forsythe took a chair beside Miriam while giving her one of his most approving and effective smiles. It was the sort which in her mother's day had made women bridle. She could feel it almost coating her with chromium plate. Branch said, "Will it be the same thing, Mr. Vanesse?"

"Yes, Branch, the same dose. Thank you, and good morning."

"Good morning, sir."

Branch left, and Forsythe opened a napkin and continued to brightly beam.

"What are you having for breakfast?" he asked.

"Kidneys."

"So am I. I always have kidneys for breakfast. When Paris stopped having kidneys I left Paris. That's me."

"What happens if we run out of them here?"

"I shall leave. I shall swim until I sink."

"Death for an ideal."

"Not at all. For a kidney. My life is operated by the mundane and the practical. A spade by me is called a spade. You don't mind my rattling on? It's the verve in the air."

"Rattle right ahead."

"It's got you, too. You look positively neon."

"That is the ravages of hunger."

"How did you sleep? With your eyes closed, I presume?"

"They were hermetically sealed. My nerves were limp, and my muscles in flaccid repose."

"Aren't you going to ask me about me?"

"If you wish.'

"Thank you, I slept fine. With the serenity of a little child."

Miriam thought: He has changed his tactics. He is treating me as a casual new acquaintance instead of as a specimen piece in schizophrenia that has to be skeletoned in the family cupboard. I wonder whether the others will also have changed theirs? Has Dr. Crowninshield ordered it? Perhaps. I'm to be dosed and simpled in the impersonal vein.

Is Forsythe the murderer? Is it he who killed Jennifer Murcheson and is planning to kill me? He looks anything but a murderer. The soundest authorities say they never do. It's no longer fashionable, if it ever was. Killers can seem the loveliest people until that flash comes, and they drop the mask and change, with their faces bare, raw death.

Forsythe said, "I say, you do look queer. A touch of the sea getting you?"

"I think it is. I think I'll consider my breakfast already eaten. If you'll give my regrets to Branch I'll go on deck for a while."

Instantly he was all concern. He sprang up and held her chair.

"I'll go with you."

"No, please, I prefer to be alone."

"But I think I should."

"I must insist, if you don't mind."

"Certainly, if you put it like that."

Miriam tried to smooth the edge off flight.

She said, "Don't let this disturb your rendezvous with the kidneys."

She caught, as she turned, his brief warm smile.

CHAPTER 11

A body impacted against Miriam as she stepped over the raised sill, caught her, steadied her.

Stone said, "I'm terribly sorry."

"It's quite all right. And good morning."

"Good morning. Sure I didn't jounce you?"

"Quite sure."

He seemed distracted, abashed almost, and at a complete loss as to what to say.

"I'm taking my morning turns of the deck."

"So many to a mile?"

"There must be. I've never figured it out. Aren't you having breakfast?"

"No."

"Feeling all right?"

"Now I am, thank you."

He gave Miriam the effect of the morning itself: chill vigor and a consuming energy of boundless spirit that suggested a kinship with the thrusting sheets of water. Wind had whipped blood richly into his cheeks, and his eyes were the darkest and clearest blue Miriam thought she had ever seen. If safety did not lie in them she did not know where it would lie. Above all else, above the confusions and undershot fears which lay damply along her nerves, she wanted this man's good regard.

She said, "I'll walk with you if you don't mind a shuttlecock for a companion. Each foot has its private idea about how to cling to the deck. Something is always in a state of suspension. Sometimes all of me."

Stone answered with the studied courtesy which had been with him last night on the dock. He offered his arm and suggested that were Miriam to take hold of it she would be all right. They started off. He had had an atrocious night with scarcely any sleep at all. He had tried everything in his power to reassure himself regarding her. To convince himself that a savant of Crowninshield's international standing could not be wrong.

It was more than that. It was this distressing personal element which was coloring (the color was rose) his every contact with this lovely creature who possessed not only the most ornamental of good looks but apparently a brain. Although this did not surprise him. Young women with the advantages of her background would have to be positive cretins to mature to her age and be moronic, whatever the dazzle of their facades. Twenty-two? She claimed, in her perversity, a twenty.

Her arm, for example, was in line with what he meant. The feel of it pressed snugly under his. Very electric, and very bad. Definitely more electrical than Elsa Davis's had been. Certainly far more so than anybody else's. But then, he had not gone in for arms. An elderly lady or two while crossing a street. Friends of his mother's in Philadelphia.

It grew evident to Miriam that Stone's comradeship during their talk on the settee of the afterdeck was dissipated.

She said impulsively, "Why are you within your wall again?"

"Am I? Sorry. Never realized I had one."

Clipped, he was getting. Clipped in his speech. As though, Miriam thought, he had weighed some problem concerning her overnight and had found her wanting. Hence this meager spraying of terseness. Must have some English blood.

"Well, you do have one. Last night I felt warm about you. You know what I mean. I felt that I was welcome, not just to sit beside you but to enter your feelings and your thoughts. I am talking like this because, as I told you then, I feel that you and Dr. Crowninshield are the only two people whom I can trust."

Stone stopped in the shelter of the deck housing on the afterdeck. The taffrail rose, stood poised, and then with a shudder swiftly fell, slicing its line across the whitened wake. Some gulls winged toughly across the sullen sky.

Stone's lips moved slightly in a smile that had no humor. He felt miserable about doing this.

"It is I who wish that I could trust you. I wish it very much."

"I'm glad of that. Pretty desperately so." Miriam placed a hand tentatively on his sleeve. "You do believe I am myself? That I am not that girl from the coast?"

He could not look at her. The miserable jumble of his feelings left his expression cold and grim.

"I am doing a dangerous, perhaps a terrible thing, if Dr. Crowninshield is right. It might upset the whole course of the treatment he has outlined. I cannot help myself. I do not want to say these things, but when I am with you I cannot help myself."

"What things?"

"First you must understand this. I told you yesterday that Dr. Crowninshield is the best man on psychiatry in the country. I said that he was as fine as anyone ever produced in Vienna. I believe that fully. I must believe it. But I must also recognize that he is over eighty years old. He is eighty-four."

"He looks sixty."

"I know. There have been certain little indications, certain small impatiences in recent months. This is not only difficult to explain but it is also treasonable to an extent to talk about it to you at all."

Miriam thought of Ida Mayford with her vagaries, which had become accented with age.

"Do you mean he is getting childish?"

"No. There is nothing drastic. It is as if his theories, which he once possessed, are now in possession of him. He is no longer the master. They are his masters. He has grown impatient with argumentative contradiction. I have been associated with him for over a year, and prior to the past few months he would have welcomed a discussion in opposition rather than have repelled one. You must remember that these momentary flare-ups are slight, are very far between."

"But they lead to what?"

"They lead to a fear on my part that he is coming to believe only such symptoms in a case as those which tend to substantiate his theories. It is more than a fear. It is a dread. Furthermore, the theories themselves have advanced to certain revolutionary points where I hesitate to follow. I do not say that this is an indisputable fact. I simply say I feel that this danger is present."

"Then you do have an open mind about my alleged condition?"

"Yes. It is the basis of my distrust in you. I cannot understand why you would be putting on this act."

Miriam felt as though he had slapped her.

"Act?"

Stone said with irritation, "You are making a fool of your relatives. That I do not mind. What I do mind, and what I will do anything to prevent, is your making a fool out of Dr. Crowninshield."

"You *believe* I am Jennifer Murcheson?"

"We know that you are. There has never been any question in my mind as to that."

"You think I am faking? Faking schizophrenia?"

"You are faking it extremely well, and for what purpose God knows. I think that if your case had come to Dr. Crowninshield's consideration previously to the past few months he would have read the small discrepancies as I have read them. He would not have refused, as he now refuses, to place them in argument. He would not have become so enthralled with his own opinions that he is pressing accepted theories beyond all previously proven bounds.

Gusts of wind filled a moment's silence, and then Stone added gently: "You must realize that possibly my whole future is now in your hands. My admissions have been unethical. I am pulled strongly in two ways. I do not want you to hurt Dr. Crowninshield by any exposure of your fraud. It would be his finish. He would face the negation of a lifetime's work. I think he would crumple up and disintegrate. And still, for your own sake, I would wish you to stop this masquerade."

"Stop it?" Miriam said fiercely. "I never began it. I've denied it. I've denounced it. You call it a masquerade, and I call it a vicious plot against my life, Dr. Stone. In plain words of single syllables, will you tell me how further I can deny it?"

"You can do so very easily. Will you?"

"Yes."

"You can admit that you are Jennifer Murcheson."

"No. Of course I can't do that. I am not Jennifer Murcheson. I am Miriam Lake, and I'm not split up. I'm intact."

He said stiffly, "I should have realized that I was wasting time."

"I think I no longer like you, Dr. Stone."

"That is quite beside the point and it cannot be helped." But it wasn't beside the point. All through him some need was crying out in Stone for this girl to like him. More than that. He would feel empty and lost without her. For a moment he viewed aghast any continuance of an existence that failed to include her somewhere near him. He had occasionally wondered how long it took to form an obsession, whether after all it were not simply the accumulative impacts of some habit. But apparently you could form one overnight. One like her.

Miriam's voice was equally stiff, if not stiffer.

"Yes, it is beside the point, Doctor. Quite."

The wind had a flat taste and all vigor seemed gone from the sea. Stone left Miriam abruptly but turned for an instant at the corner of the deck housing and regarded her with a look in which the pressure of some profound longing seemed to battle with distaste.

Miriam felt no urge to follow him, to probe any further among his perplexities concerning herself. She realized with a sense of despair that she no longer felt anything in regard to Stone at all. This void (where formerly she had felt such lively interest) shut him off within an impersonal obscurancy. Something, she thought, in the manner of the cerements that shroud the dead.

CHAPTER 12

Luncheon was determinedly kind.

Donald Murcheson and Mrs. Vanesse both offered the same beamish front to Miriam which Forsythe had affected at breakfast, or rather at her lack of breakfast. Crowninshield had been bolstered by a good night's sleep which had lasted well into the late morning. He almost glittered with professional interest in Miriam behind his pince-nez, while his beard seemed to glow. Stone alone presented a granite face and consciously avoided ever looking at her.

It was Mrs. Vanesse who had come to Miriam's cabin and had insisted upon her joining them in the dining saloon. Murcheson had held her chair out after wishing her the kindest of good mornings and looking at her with warm sympathy in his dark brown glassy eyes.

Murcheson did not sit down. Instead, he picked up a glass of light wine which was being served with the melon.

"I am going to propose a toast. To Miriam, and our happiness at having her among us—at lunch."

The others stood. Even Crowninshield (his knees) got laboriously to his feet. Miriam glanced at Stone and thought: He looks as though the wine were going to choke him, as if it had been personally poured out by a Borgia. She felt covered with a strange confusion. For many years she had come to consider toast-offerers as imbeciles.

But the confusion was deeper than the normal one of being toasted. She sensed in Murcheson's manner a trueness of feeling and of good intention. It swept her back fifteen years and more to childhood memories of her father, when the family would dine *en fete*. He also had been a toaster. Forsythe was seated at Miriam's left.

He said, "Why do people always flush when they're being toasted? They either flush or simper. Myself, I've never been toasted. It's one of my hidden dreams. Someday I shall tell you the rest of them. They ought to get a book out listing toastees, like *Who's Who*."

"Segregating the flushers from the simperers?"

"You have caught the idea neatly. You are also looking far better than you did this morning. That emerald patina has gone from your face."

"The same cause remains. It's been intensified."

"The ravages of hunger?"

"Yes. How were your kidneys?"

"Never mind. I'll let you in on a news item. We're having muscovy duck."

"Let me in still further. What makes it muscovy?"

"How sweet such innocence! It's the red carunculations about the beast's eyes and forehead."

"Just a duck with a noble Russian brow."

"I didn't say noble, and they've nothing whatever to do with the Soviet. Their habitat ranges from Mexico, which I do *not* pronounce Mehico, to southern Brazil. In its uncorrupted state the name was musk duck."

"Then corruption does have its charms."

"Always. May I point out further examples?"

"No."

"I'll pout."

"Go ahead and pout. I want to eat."

Miriam ate and thought: He can't be a murderer. He's much too frothy. He's a soufflé. Well, how about the De Medicis? Hadn't they also had their frothy moments? Their passages of wit? Why should sparkle be a deterrent to murder? It wasn't. Murder with a fizz. So he killed her effervescently.

How about trueness of feeling and good intention? How about Mr. Donald Murcheson? Mercy killings could lie in his repertoire. Old Euthanasia Murcheson. The sympathetic eye and the comforting hand as it pressed the dagger in. The: "This hurts me more than it does you, and it will hurt me for longer, dear girl, because just in about one jiffy while *I* am still suffering *you* will be picking out celestial chords-for-beginners on a brand-new harp."

What about Mrs. Vanesse? According to Leclos she was a woman with a terrible problem burdening her bosom. And what a bosom. How did that state of affairs shape up as a block to a murderous pass? Was not a heart-gnawing burden the prima-facie prod to innumerable murders?

Miriam was a great believer in the strength of her own sex. A frank advocate of the weakness of the male. There wasn't a male who couldn't have his hair cut, let the pillars of the temple fall later where they might. This whole charade in chicanery could easily have had its inception in a Delilah's mind. In Mrs. Vanesse's mind. With her son and her brother well-cropped into complaisance by her shears.

Miriam observed Mrs. Vanesse while packing away the muscovy duck, which tasted like any other well-cooked duck. Mrs. Vanesse faced her across the table, at Murcheson's right. She was engaged in a lively running commentary on spies-she-had-almost-unmasked with Crownin-shield who was seated on her left and who wasn't listening to her at all.

"There was that foreign houseman" (Mrs. Vanesse said) "of Greta Norworth's. Greta was positive he was a Nazi because his *rs* had that guttural, growling sound. Like a chest cold. It's quite unmistakable, and so different from the clipped French purr. He lived over the garage, and every afternoon when she turned on the news broadcast it was simply drowned out by this local interference, so she burst into his room one day and the fact that it was an electric razor only proved his cunning. He was in shorts and had those distinctively Prussian-officer legs. Greta was positive that the electric razor was only camouflage to cover the times when he actually did use his short-wave transmitter, and said so."

Crowninshield murmured abstractedly, "And was it?"

"Greta never did find out. The man gave notice and left the same afternoon. He had the impudence to suggest that she take a weekend off and spend it at Bellevue. Then there was that French maid of Alfreda Borden's. Definitely in the worst phase of pro-Nazi Vichy. She never actually went so far as to *heil* Alfreda in the morning, but she looked it, and Alfreda said that her arm movement when she pulled the portieres open was a positive Nazi salute."

Mrs. Vanesse (Miriam thought) is talking under forced draft. She knows that Dr. Crowninshield isn't paying the least attention. Leclos is right. Mrs. Vanesse is cruelly, desperately worried over something. She is watching me guardedly, watching everything I do. And she is watching her son. She listened to his chatter with me, to each inconsequential word of it.

Then Forsythe was speaking to her and (Miriam noted) Mrs. Vanesse was listening in again.

"The last time I had these ducks," Forsythe said, "was on a plane. There was something rather poignant about it. To be in flight and eat the bird—" His voice faltered, and blood drained swiftly from his face. "Mother—good God—"

A glass clashed against china as Mrs. Vanesse gave a small inarticulate cry, like a child faced with sudden and appalling terror, and fell forward in a dead faint.

CHAPTER 13

Mrs. Vanesse, after she was restored, refused to give any explanation of her faint other than that she was subject to spells. There was nothing the matter with her, nothing at all. She would go below and rest for a while. She would be perfectly all right. Perfectly.

There was no further lunch. Leclos, summoned, assisted Mrs. Vanesse below to her cabin, and Crowninshield made no bones about offering his arm to Miriam and suggesting that they retire to the library, where it would be quiet. For a little talk.

He expressed concern over Mrs. Vanesse after they were settled.

"She is dosing herself with sedatives for her nerves," he said. "That is stupid. She is carrying a burden wrapped up within herself. What it is I do not know. No one can know, because if she had unburdened herself by confession she would not be now on the verge of a dangerous breakdown. There is no doubt as to that. I have asked her to share this burden with me under the strictest cloak of professional secrecy. To do so would relieve her as surely as though she had purged from her system some malignant poison. She refused. As a defense, she tells me that I do not know what I am talking about."

Crowninshield begged Miriam to savor the absurdity of such a thing with a smile that glinted pale pink lips over his beard.

"Doctor, this isn't rudeness when I say that I agree with Mrs. Vanesse. At least in so far as your diagnosis of me is concerned."

Crowninshield brushed this aside as being totally inconsequential.

"I would be deeply surprised if your attitude were otherwise. And now we must get on. You slept last night?"

"Yes."

"You dreamed?"

"No, Doctor."

"Then tell me of your thoughts. Tell me in infinite detail of your slightest ones."

"That would be a piece of impertinence on my part, because of the falseness of the whole structure you have built up about me. I can't do it, Doctor."

"I am patient. It is perhaps the quintessence of my chosen field of research to be so. There are endless days before us. We can be spendthrifts with time."

Miriam thought: I am being stupid. I am in danger, as desperately in danger as that note described: murder is its root. Surely my sole defense is knowledge? To know as much about this girl as I can discover, this girl who is so surely dead? Then perhaps through a reconstruction of that crime I can unmask her murderer before he murders me. If I can state with even a partial chance of convincing anyone: "Jennifer Murcheson is dead and here is the man who killed her," then surely I will find allies who will be willing to believe me to be myself.

Miriam observed the placid repose into which Crowninshield had settled, the calm waxy hands, the gentle movement of his lavender silk tie with every breath. A bearded sphinx in reverse. One eager to receive secrets rather than dispense them. Everything was there except for his haunches squatting in a field of sand.

"Doctor, will you tell me something?"

"Certainly."

"You said last night that you were in possession of my case history. That is, of the case history of Jennifer Murcheson."

"I am."

"Will you tell it to me? Will you tell me everything about that girl?"

"I shall, and I shall not conceal from you that I am pleased. This curiosity is of the greatest significance. It shows a healthy awakening of your subconscious and an effort on the part of Jennifer Murcheson to *get through*. You already are aware that 'she' is the niece of Mr. Murcheson and of Mrs. Vanesse."

"Yes."

"She is the daughter—would it distress you if I were to change that 'she' to 'you'? Does the thought repel you?"

"It does, but I have no objection. My concern is to learn the facts."

Crowninshield made a brief purring sound as if in pleasure at a point-in-contest gained.

"Then I shall say 'you.' Your father was Bellamy Murcheson, the eldest of the three Murcheson heirs. Through him you inherited the largest portion of the Murcheson fortune, which prior to his death he had converted into securities of the safest if of the most fluid nature. I mean that they can almost be said to have the attributes of ready cash. According to the physician who attended his final illness and was present at the end, your father warned you almost with his dying breath to 'sit tight on the boodle and not let any of those damned eastern coyotes or any banks or investment-counsel pirates get their hooks into it.'"

"Isn't there a case something like that in the courts now? I think I read of it. A Philadelphia woman's estate?"

"Yes. That case involves eighteen millions and has been in litigation for five years. It will have to go on for at least five more years before all of the contestants' claims are heard. It is odd your speaking of it, because that woman became very very much the same sort of a recluse that you became."

"I think Mr. Bellamy Murcheson must have been a rather curious man."

"He was. I might say that in addition to his fortune you also inherited a good many of his traits."

"I trust they were admirable, Doctor?"

Crowninshield sent her a suspicious glance and said, "With men of your father's financial standing all traits have a habit of being admirable. Headstrong aptitudes become transmuted from mere mulishness into the jaw-juttings of a Caesar. Tendencies toward emotional excesses, ones which swing between a prankish love of crowds and a hermit urge profound in its craving for isolation, are considered to be admirably right: the mettlesome fire and brooding reserve of a blooded horse."

(I'm a mule, Miriam thought. I'm a horse.)

"And so," Crowninshield went on, "there was nothing remarkable in the isolation within which you fenced yourself on the ranch in southern California following your father's death."

"When did his death occur, Doctor?"

"Six years ago last April."

"Just how exact was Miss Murcheson's isolation?"

"It amounted virtually to a retreat from the social and outside worlds. Again I can suggest its similarity to the case you spoke about of the woman in Philadelphia."

"People thought her poor, didn't they? Didn't she live in almost a miserly simplicity?"

"That is possible. I do not know. It was not so, however, in your case. You continued in the rather grand manner which had pleased your father."

"But with no banking account—"

"My dear Miss Murcheson, you simply motored into Los Angeles and sold a bond. Your father's former bank there grew perfectly accustomed to your habit of doing so. I have explained that all your securities were as negotiable as cash."

"Then there were no business contacts, no financial obligations which required signatures?"

"None."

"What of friends?"

"You discouraged all friends by repeatedly and rudely refusing to see them when they called. Your obvious desire was to erase all former ties with the completeness of a sponged-off slate. Your staff of servants was replaced by Mexicans hired and imported by you personally. You must see that even as far back as that period, six years ago, you were subconsciously tending to *become someone else*."

"Surely she must have gone off on trips? Have done something?"

"No. You had traveled too frequently with your father. He had always taken you with him, abroad, into wildernesses, wherever he went. For you to have gone on any voyage after his death would have kept fresh too keenly your grief. The ranch is a large one running into thousands of acres. In itself it is a miniature domain. You were not idle. Your interest turned toward Mexican art. You became proficient in pottery-making."

How clearly, Miriam thought, was the design falling into sinister shape. That isolated girl, possessed of a large fortune, self-imprisoned from her friends, unfettered by the servants of her childhood days. For years quietly satisfied with her chosen absorption of pottery-making. And then she was dead from murder, and the motive was stark: the major portion of the Murcheson wealth. Or were all of these surmises too simple because of their complete obviousness?

Crowninshield had permitted the pause to lengthen. His eyes never left Miriam. He unfolded his hands and rested them on his knees, palms up. Pale china leaves.

He said, "And then you disappeared."

"In what fashion?"

"A disappearance precludes any fashion, Miss Murcheson."

"Possibly for purists, Doctor. I should have asked what steps preceded the vanishing?"

"You followed your usual morning custom of riding the mountain trails after breakfast, a habit you had never varied from since childhood. Neither you nor your horse came back."

"Naturally there was a search?"

"Naturally. One that broadened through the county and the state. One that eventually took in the nation and abroad."

"I recall no publicity about it in the papers."

"There was none. The search was privately subscribed for by your uncle. The Durney people conducted it. There are no better. The initial conjecture was that you had been kidnapped, but there were never any demands for ransom, and this idea was shortly discarded."

"Why not amnesia? Why do you not even now consider a simple case of amnesia rather than this diagnosis of schizophrenia? This remains an argument in the abstract, Doctor."

"That is a premise you naturally insist upon my maintaining."

"Suppose Miss Murcheson had been thrown from her horse? Struck her head? Could not that have caused amnesia?

"My dear Miss Murcheson, there was no horse. The horse, too, had disappeared. Certainly amnesia was considered, but the Durney people dispelled the probability."

"How?"

"With amnesia of the retrograde type your memory would have been a blank on everything prior to the injury which caused it. When consciousness returned you would have followed the habitually routine habit of professing this loss of memory to the person or people who came to your assistance. Almost invariably this would have led to your being taken to someone in authority, to a hospital, and your case would have become one of record. The Durney people investigated that angle with a thoroughness that left no doubt."

"This is very confusing. I fail to see the difference. If it was schizo-phrenia—"

Crowninshield broke in with the impatient sharpness of triumph.

"There is no 'if.' There *was no loss of memory*. You became this other self, this Miriam Lake, in every detail. Complete with a past and a present and with this Miriam Lake's full appetites of life. Smoking is one excellent example. As Jennifer Murcheson tobacco was abhorrent to *you*. As Miriam Lake you find it pleasing. One of the most perfect schizophrenic splits I have ever encountered."

"Doctor, it is absurd to believe that I could supply myself with a full-grown past. That the endless memories of my childhood, my real childhood, could be ready-manufactured. I maintain that that is almost pathologically absurd."

"Certainly you do."

"You are believing such things as you wish to believe. All of this. All of your extraordinary inventions."

A flash of anger marred Crowninshield's placid face. It was quickly erased.

He said equably, "I have been accused of having become increasingly impatient of criticism during the past year by Dr. Stone. If I have, it is because I am convinced that my conclusions based on a lifetime of work are no longer subject either to speculation or doubt. I have gone many steps farther into this shadowland of the brain than any of my con-temporaries, certainly a good deal farther than the hidebound authorities of the past, than their first tentative fumblings. A few of my conclusions are considered revolutionary." He smiled sweetly again "I am happy to admit that they are."

"Did Miss Murcheson also assume complete economic potentialities in her new state?"

"Your mind continues to be excitingly acute. You undoubtedly took with you as many securities as you pleased from the vault at the ranch. A vault, I must reassure you, which has been under capable guard since your disappearance was learned of."

"How was Miss Murcheson finally found? I mean why the choice of me?"

"Your general description was obtained from the servants at the ranch. There were no photographs more recent than those taken in your childhood. A hermit has small use for portraits of himself."

"Why didn't this description come from Mr. Murcheson or Mrs. Vanesse?"

"Neither had seen you since your father's funeral six years ago. You were then a girl of sixteen. You were determined. You were willfully headstrong. You were exceptionally mature for your age. Again, your father's traits."

"Something of a problem child."

"Very much of one. At the funeral you were openly antagonistic to your uncle and your aunt, both of whom you asserted had never understood your father, and certainly had never approved of him. You placed them with delicate but unmistakable implications among the brood of birds called vultures."

"That would seem to be very plain speaking."

"It was. You were aware of the contemptuous hostility which your father had always felt toward his brother, whom he considered an idealistic fool, and toward his sister, who was in his opinion a silly Francophile, one who was bringing her son Forsythe up to be an enameled frog. The phraseology was his."

"I wish I had known him."

Crowninshield twittered.

"Good. Again you are trying to come through. Well, there it was. You did not see your uncle or your aunt or your cousin again after the funeral until you came on board last night."

"Why, as the name of Murcheson was used in the letters to me—why wouldn't it have recalled that other self?"

"The name Murcheson bears no more significance to your present self than does the name of Smith. This you must believe: so deep, so thick, so opaque is the curtain"

"All right, Doctor. The Durney people had Jennifer Murcheson's description. Then what?"

"Their methods are myriad. Obviously they include the personal columns and the classified advertisements in the newspapers. Obviously they employ the medium themselves by inserting 'Wanted' advertisements covering most fields of work. That is but one of their many methods. In your, case it was the one that worked."

Yes, it had worked: Woman Wanted, and then a flexible set of requirements as to age and background which Miriam had felt could have been stretched into applicability to herself. And an equally flexible set of inducements that had been tempting.

"The business connected with that advertisement was conducted solely by letter, Doctor."

"So you were led to believe. You were covertly observed, as were all of the other applicants. The resemblance to your general physical description was impressive. Your letters were taken to a handwriting expert for his opinion. He is satisfied that your writing checks with that of a scathing note sent by you six years ago, after your father's funeral to your cousin Forsythe just before he and his mother returned to France."

Yes, that would have been attended to also. The plot was too competently mortised to permit of a detail of such importance being overlooked. Far too much money was involved to risk any substitution on a chance of resemblance in physical looks. You could do almost anything with enough money. You could make people lie and steal and forge and kill. You could make them love and hate. Always, somewhere, you could buy a tool who would do any of such things.

"How many girls other than myself were considered, Doctor?"

"Throughout the past year, while the search was being made? My dear Miss Murcheson, I believe they numbered hundreds."

Miriam thought: And then I came along. I not only looked enough like Jennifer Murcheson but I otherwise fitted the bill. Alone, no family, and no close friends. Ripe to vanish. The murderer had indeed been a careful, patient man. And at last he was rewarded. He was rewarded by getting me.

"Doctor, has it ever been considered that Jennifer Murcheson is dead?"

Crowninshield dismissed the question as too elemental for discussion.

"Apart from the facts that your horse was never found, that your body was never found, there was the immediate consideration that you had been brought up in the closest sort of association with an incipient megalomaniac. Your father. Universally it is accepted that the trait is not inheritable. I am not a bigot. I accept no dogma simply because it has received the accolade of universal favor. Tomatoes were once shuddered at as being poisonous. The fashion in diets reverses itself as frequently as that of women's hats. A thousand examples. Even dismissing the inheritance angle, the mind of a child is plastic, a soft plate on which propinquity can etch. As your father etched upon yours. No, you are not dead, Miss Murcheson. You are in the grip of a malady of which it is my business to cure you. Before it is too late."

"Too late?"

"There are certain dangers."

"So you said last night. You dismissed suicide."

"You misunderstood me. I dismissed it as a probable result of anger. I am far from satisfied that any sudden aggravation of your condition might not lead to it. An opinion which I have freely shared with the others. It is, however, the danger which I consider least likely."

"I am in danger from what else, Doctor?"

"You? Again you misunderstand me. Your personal safety is in danger from nothing whatever, Miss Murcheson. On the contrary. Unless you bend every effort to comply willingly with my course of treatment you could become a potential danger to others. Any emotional intensification—"

"Danger to others?" (The plot with sickening swiftness was taking on new and terrible potentialities.) "Your serious belief is that I might harm somebody?"

"You must be told the gravity of your state. You must accept the ultimate of its dire importance. Otherwise you would continue to rebel against placing yourself in my hands. Yes, Miss Murcheson, the moment might come when you would even kill."

CHAPTER 14

It was obvious that Crowninshield felt a period had been reached for the day. He pressed himself upright, carefully, with his hands on the arms of the chair.

He said, "I shall stop now with this one request. Strange thoughts will come to you throughout the day and night. Do not disbar them. Remember them. In the morning, out of their tortuous mass, I shall select such ones which may serve as levers for my job. Your mind is in a turmoil. I want it to be so. Only by direct and disturbingly forceful blows can the defensive wall of your present being be pierced." His voice grew less didactic. "Do not be too distressed. Accept this milieu which of necessity seems forced upon you. Find pleasure in it. Taste of that love, that sympathy which surrounds you."

They left the library and stood for a while on deck, observing in silence the increased power of the sea, the ridges of the mounting waves, gray chargers beneath a metal-capping sky. Crowninshield said that he would go below and rest. More and more of late he had come to feel the need of relaxation for an hour or so after lunch. He supposed it a tribute exacted by his years. He went inside.

Miriam walked to the afterdeck. She felt battered and frightened to the point of illness.

Mrs. Vanesse was occupying the settee in the shelter of the deck housing. She sat, in a warm woolen coat, unrelaxed. Her importantly bosomed torso seemed to combat rather than yield to the movement of the yacht. She was knitting a military sock with the swift and mechanical accuracy of an automaton. Her badly penciled lips were set in a thin line and her eyes, when she looked up at Miriam, were similarly hard with some strong emotion. They awoke in Miriam an immediate sense of pity.

"I do hope you are better, Mrs. Vanesse."

"Thank you. I am quite all right again. This air is finishing the cure. Do you find it chilly?"

"No."

"Then won't you sit down?"

The commonplace suggestion held an undercurrent of tense urgency. Miriam found discomfort in this hinted tension. There was a turning point about it. The sort of odd premonition which you sometimes feel when faced with making the most ordinary of decisions. In this instance, whether to sit down with Mrs. Vanesse or to keep walking around the deck and go below. The reluctance grew into a foreboding of danger out of all proportion to the relative simplicity of the request. No danger from the immediate moment but one which later would accrue, would announce its climax at the end of a powder chain which would be ignited by this act of sitting down.

Mrs. Vanesse no longer concealed the urgency in her voice.

"Please do. I have the oddest attack of loneliness. Do they ever come to you?"

Miriam sat down on the settee.

"I'm sure they do to everybody."

"They must. With me it's most infrequent. Just as some people seem immune to the ordinary illnesses. Headache, dyspepsia, that sort of thing. Loneliness could be classed as an illness, don't you think?"

"Yes, in the sense that there are many remedies for it."

"No, not always." Mrs. Vanesse's eyes remained fixed on her knitting. "I have known when there were none."

With an increasing discomfiture of nerves Miriam saw Mrs. Vanesse glance furtively to right and left as though to assure herself that the deck (which obviously was so) was empty.

"I remember being appalled one day as a child," Mrs. Vanesse went on. "I had a very dear friend of my own age which was seven. An Edna Waycombe. It was one of those lifelong friendships that are common among children, filled with new and rare extravagances. Like little boys becoming blood brothers with thoroughly unantiseptic rites of pricking out drops of blood and so forth. Edna and I did not go so far as that, but there were vows—oh, you know the sort of thing I mean."

"I know them very well."

"One day Edna became a thief. She stole a large heart-shaped silver locket from a mutual friend, a Beatrice Shaftsbury, aged six. The value of the locket was negligible, but the act itself struck a deathblow in my heart. I still loved Edna. I could not help keeping on doing that, but I had the most terrifying sort of nightmares and would wake up screaming, night after night. They revolved around punishment in brimstone, as my Sunday school teacher had only recently acquainted me with the punitive measures reputed to be *an fait* in hell. I don't see why I should go on boring you with this."

Miriam did not want Mrs. Vanesse to stop. She felt it was not an anecdote which Mrs. Vanesse was telling, rather that it was an allegory, an indirect method of conveying some guidepost to the burden which was weighing the older woman down.

"No, Mrs. Vanesse. Do go on."

"Well, there was Edna being boiled in brimstone in my dreams for her sin, and my days became haggard because Edna did not know that I knew. I had the conviction that if I were to admit this, then Edna would do something drastic along a child's conception of suicide. The one most in favor among my set was a watery grave. The next stop to which being, of course, the pot of brimstone. I finally did end up by telling Edna I knew. I did so in the assured hope that she would return the locket to Beatrice and would thus, after due repentance, palliate her future punishment into something more tepid."

"And did she?"

"No, my dear, she did not. She slapped both Beatrice and me so soundly that we were speechless with hysteria. She declared a flat intention of keeping the locket and a determination to scratch out our four eyes and feed them to the cat if either of us betrayed her with a word."

"A most interesting child."

"Unquestionably. But I could not, at seven, take any maturely dispassionate or cynical point of view about it. The cat's proposed dinner held both Beatrice and me in a sweat of terror for many months, and it only abated when Edna's family moved her with them to Boston. The point is this, if there is any point. I tasted loneliness for the first time of the type for which there is no remedy. My trust, my love, had been crushed under what seemed to be an insensate heel, and my world was emptied of everyone but myself. I was alone."

Miriam thought: There is some application of that occurrence which is pertinent today. Right now to the present moment. A pertinence that pertains to Jennifer Murcheson and so, through substitution, to me.

"Mrs. Vanesse, I have known you for a very short while. To all purposes we have only just met one another. I think you want to tell me something. Won't you be more direct?"

"No. There is nothing. I have nothing to tell you. But there is something I would like to ask."

"Yes?"

Mrs. Vanesse again glanced furtively to right and left and then looked at Miriam with an expression that was almost tangible from its intensity.

"Tell me—tell me this—have you ever had a mole removed? They can be, you know."

"I know they can."

"Well? From the base of the neck—right here? A small mole, scarcely a blemish, and my memory of it is of the vaguest. Something one thinks one remembers and then begins to wonder whether the thought, by repetition, might not have given birth to a false memory? Please think. Please tell me. Probably in Los Angeles or San Francisco?"

The unreal aspects of Miriam's arrival on board the night before were, she decided, on the expand. A mole. Always with the princess-in-rags motif there was a mole. No matter what else would be lost her, she, the princess, retained her mole. This then would be identified at the nadir of her varied miseries and would translate her back into her regal state of ermine, frosted cakes, and the best-looking prince still loose.

"I have never," Miriam said, "been to Los Angeles or San Francisco. I have never had an operation for a mole." Her answer plunged Mrs. Vanesse into a moment of profound dejection, and then she looked at Miriam with a combined sorrow and terror that was unmistakable. So strongly were these two emotions indicated that Miriam shrank back.

The gesture brought Mrs. Vanesse to herself, and she said rapidly, "No—do not shrink from me. I am a confused, a desperately harassed woman. I am certain now that my memory was false." She closed her eyes as if to black out some picture too wretchedly sinister to contemplate. She said, "There was no mole."

"I think that there was. I think that you know I am not Jennifer Murcheson."

"No, that is not true. You are my niece. There is every proof that you are."

"I think that Jennifer Murcheson is dead. Perhaps murdered."

Mrs. Vanesse cried, "Don't say that! Oh, my dear, can't you see that that is impossible?"

"I think it perfectly probable, Mrs. Vanesse."

The older woman dropped her knitting and gripped one of Miriam's wrists very hard. She leaned close to Miriam and said with passionate earnestness, "Child, that shadowland into which your brain is plunged is cloudy with fevered dreams. I beg of you to dismiss them." Then she added swiftly in sudden contradiction to this wish: "Tell me, you think that I, or my brother, or my son—?"

"What else can I think?"

"You can let me dispel the thought forever from your mind. Shall I give you proof?"

"Yes."

"On that day a year ago when you disappeared, Forsythe, Donald, and I were in the East. We were distant from your ranch in California by three thousand miles."

"Were you together in New York, Mrs. Vanesse?"

"I was staying at the Waldorf. Forsythe and I had landed two weeks before from Lisbon. On the day before you disappeared, Donald had gone to Boston for the week end to settle some final matters concerning his foundation for social research. That was on a Saturday. He returned from Boston on Monday. I remember that we lunched at the Colony Restaurant. That steak thing Donald likes, with the sauce."

"And your son?"

"Forsythe was away for the week end also. I have some property in Virginia, and he had gone down to see what the possibilities were for arranging a sale. He returned on time on Monday to join Donald and me at luncheon. He advised that we hold on to the Virginia place a little longer, as the real-estate people he talked with while down there thought that later in the year the property could be sold to a club. It was not until the following Sunday, Jennifer, that we learned you had vanished."

Mrs. Vanesse released her grip on Miriam's wrist and swiftly picked up her knitting. The needles clicked desperately in her fingers. Her face was ashen.

Murcheson had just turned the corner of the deck housing. He stopped in front of them. He said quietly, "You look cold, Kate. Your cheeks are livid. Hadn't you better go below and lie down?"

Mrs. Vanesse managed a smile with lips that trembled.

"Yes, Donald. Perhaps I had."

CHAPTER 15

The balance of the afternoon, and dinner, and the evening hours offered no moments of subsequent importance. None, that is, that was visibly apparent. Until the hour between eleven o'clock and midnight, which Miriam spent with Stone in the main saloon.

Mrs. Vanesse had retired early, at ten. Miriam knew her to have been under an excessive strain, a strain which Mrs. Vanesse had made every effort to conceal beneath a set social manner. Crowninshield had declined bridge and had followed Mrs. Vanesse below shortly afterwards. Forsythe and Murcheson had played backgammon until eleven and then had said good night, leaving Miriam to finish a game of Russian bank with Stone.

It had been a curious game, one played with a polite and granite reserve on Stone's part and with a coldly precise exactitude by Miriam. Both of these attitudes were but outer coverings to their true feelings, which could best be summed up as an armistice among their warring emotions. Neither had cared to play Russian bank (and decidedly not together), but each had accepted the game as a medium for establishing this inner truce.

Miriam had made up her mind far earlier in the day that as she was compelled to live out the immediate present in this total nightmare, there was nothing to be gained by small and inconsequential rebellions. She would follow with constant guard and awareness such stuffs as the dream was made of.

But this was not simple for her to do with Stone.

Her feelings toward Stone were at least resolved. She had been familiar with the irrational fevers and seesaw temperature changes of love and realized damned well that she was getting them again because of him. She knew that they would make her ridiculous and unhappy, and would throw her into the worst sort of attitudinzing, one far beyond the poise proper to a reasoning human being, while he would continue to regard her as a whited sepulcher of sorts, if that would cover his belief in her being a young woman of wealth who for her own devious reasons was going in for an outrageous psychopathical sham. A sham that aimed dangerously at his idol, the already teetering Crowninshield. Instead of what she was. A plain girl in plain danger being detestably exploited for purposes of someone's profit. A proxy for a corpse.

Miriam had considered Mrs. Vanesse's talk of the afternoon and had dismissed it as unsound so far as the value of any alibi was concerned. The three of them had been separated on the day of Jennifer Murcheson's disappearance and on the days preceding and following it: Donald Murcheson in Boston, Mrs. Vanesse in New York, and Forsythe Vanesse in Virginia. Presumably. The mileage to California meant nothing. Any one of them could have taken a night plane on Saturday, have spent Sunday at the ranch in California (murdering Jennifer), and have taken a Sunday-night plane back to be on hand for the reunion at lunch in the Colony Restaurant on Monday.

Unless there had been sufficient witnesses in Boston, New York, and Virginia to prove the alibi of each of them.

What Miriam could not dismiss had been Mrs. Vanesse's manner. The woman had been in the grip of some soul-shaking emotion. Unquestionably she had wanted to confer some message to Miriam, a desire which Murcheson's sudden appearance had checked. Had not only checked but which had driven Mrs. Vanesse into a spasm of pallid fear.

Stone won the game of Russian bank. The hour had been a torment. Any number of times he had wanted to throw his cards down on the table and leave the saloon. Flee from it, really. And from her. His obsession (it had become one by now) had even reached the fantastic stage where wonderings had popped up as to what things she did and did not like. A domestic touch. A picture only too perilously backgrounded by an altar. Her probable tastes in music and in food. In books. She would like Wodehouse. That was simple. But how about Joseph Conrad? Was that too much to ask? He brushed mad follies aside.

He said with the most conventional consideration, "Are you tired?"

"Yes"

(Thank God.)

"Then shall we go below?"

"Not unless you want to turn in."

"No, not a bit. What would you like to do?"

"Sit here and talk for a while, I think."

Stone gathered up cards and arranged them methodically into their separate packs while every ounce of sound and analytically scientific sense urged him to fight.

He said, "I want to thank you, incidentally."

"For what?"

"For not having disclosed to Dr. Crowninshield my opinions concerning his condition."

"Had you thought that I would?"

"I did not know. I am not a confidant of your plans."

"They're very simple. They consist in a determination to get off this boat at the earliest moment I can. Preferably under my own motive power."

"What do you mean by that?"

"I mean not in a wooden box."

"Your thoughts are on death?"

"On murder, Doctor."

It occurred instantly to Miriam that this was a foolish thing to have said. With Mrs. Vanesse she had not been able to help herself, for she had felt that Mrs. Vanesse had been on the verge of making some disclosure which had required just such a prodding to break down her reserves. But with Stone it was different.

Stone had nothing to disclose. Certainly no such torment as the one which gnawed at Mrs. Vanesse. Even if Miriam were to discuss her whole construction of the plot with him, as she interpreted it. Stone would simply swing rapidly to Crowninshield's opinion and agree that her brain was truly affected. Everyone (including Stone) would be very kind about it, and Mrs. Vanesse and her brother and her son would spread out their several and perfect alibis for the three days surrounding Jennifer's disappearance.

Miriam now regretted tremendously having spoken of her suspicions to Mrs. Vanesse. Would Mrs. Vanesse keep still, or would she discuss the matter with her brother and her son? The murderer would definitely be put upon his guard (Mrs. Vanesse herself might be the murderess) and would feel impelled to hasten the arranging for that secret moment when he could overpower Miriam and throw her into the sea. Stone was continuing to observe her thoughtfully.

He said, "I find you very difficult to understand. I find a most unsensible desire to believe the things you say. I do not like this sudden new line on murder."

"It fails to enchant me also."

"I wish you would tell me more."

Miriam saw that he was getting his professional look. It was a relief from the granite one. She felt a want to encourage it, because it obviously seemed to make him more personally aware of her even if only as an interesting meal for mental degustation. A nice word. When you could get it. Obsolete, Webster called it. And what of it?

"How many times does a word not have to be used in order for it to become obsolete?"

"Do not wander, please. I am interested in this train of thought of yours on murder."

And I, my dead-pan bucko, have entered the silly season and am interested in your raven gloomish hair. Look here (Miriam thought), I must snap out of this. The man is becoming a solvent. Everything melts away around him like the furniture and strong noises of the sea. What a job you could do on him at the domestic breakfast table.

"Murder was just a thought, Doctor. Call it idle."

"It was not idle. I've sense enough for that. I want to know what was at the bottom of it."

A lingering hope that it was he who had sent the note of warning caused Miriam to say impulsively, "Murder is its root."

The phrase obviously meant nothing to Stone beyond sharpening his professional look to a point of needle keenness.

"Very well. Go on."

"That's all."

"This is extremely irritating."

"Do you think that you have the proper equanimity for your chosen field of work, Doctor?"

He answered her quite seriously.

"I am beginning to think that I have not. I have begun to wonder about it. Your case has distressed me as sharply as it has interested me. I say that in spite of my doubts of which I have told you. They are still with me. I still do not believe in your condition."

"That's half a cake anyhow."

"My difficulty lies in not being able to hold an analytically impersonal point of view. You refuse to stay set in the abstract. From the very start you were much more of a person than a problem. I felt so on the dock, and while you were sitting beside me in the tender with the fog shutting us out from all other things. It's bad. It is very bad."

"Isn't there some serum among the antitoxins?"

"You laugh at me. Naturally. I assure you that I find no humor in it."

"The mirth is hollow, Doctor."

Stone said irritably, "There are too many shades, too many nuances. They obscure the clarity of truth just when you feel you are about to view it. There is no point in our pursuing this further tonight. I am hungry. I would like some roast-beef sandwiches and beer. Do you suppose there would be such a thing? I've lost my first edge for the novelty of endless pates on thin bread and wine."

"I can think of nothing better. They'd have no roast beef cooked, but possibly there is some in cans. Why not ring?"

"You will stay here? You will join me?"

"I will match you bite with bite."

"You are wonderful when you're like this. You don't mind my saying that, do you?"

"About as much so as a Barrymore is appalled by applause."

Stone rang.

He threw discretion to the winds. He told her, over sandwiches, a good deal about himself. His parents were living in the old house in Philadelphia where he had been born, and where his father had been born. His father owned silk mills in Paterson and considered Stone's choice of psychiatry for a career much in the same attitude as a hen has who has unaccountably hatched a duck egg. But the old fellow had been reasonable and had shifted the entire blame onto Stone's mother. Some quirk in her ancestry.

It was midnight before the sandwiches were finished and they went below. At her cabin door Stone said good night, and Miriam went inside feeling normally refreshed for the first moment since she had been on board.

Biddle had already turned down the bed and arranged her nightgown, wrapper, and slippers. Sandwiches were again on a silver tray, and the small pitcher of milk. Biddle had left the bed lamp turned on. The foreign correspondent's diary was on the bed table, with a matchstick where she had marked her place in it the night before.

Miriam bolted the door and with an almost total relaxation from nervous worry undressed and took a warm bath. The motion of the water in the tub was far more violent than it had been the night before, and one sea which the *Donna Louise* headed into sent water sheeting over the bath's rim onto the floor. Even this did not disturb Miriam's almost hypnotic sense of peace. Stone stayed in her mind. Tucked there. As something treasurably hoarded to be taken out at will and glimpsed. A miser's gold. Or an Ickes' canful of gasoline.

Flames.

Surely there would be some police investigation of the fire which had destroyed the cottage. They would at least learn that it was rented by a Miss Miriam Lake. Hope blazed for an instant and then died. Her happily garlicked and accented neighbors would grin their enchanting grins and tell any inquiring cop: No know. Much away. Always by herself. Very foolish woman. No young gent friends. No bambinos. Very nice but I think she is crazy like mad. Sure she have car. Car gone? Okay, then she gone too.

Which little deduction would save the police from the bother of sifting the ashes of the ruins for her bones.

Miriam put on her nightgown. She had some difficulty in doing this due to the occasional violent plunges taken by the yacht. She sat on the edge of the bed. The great solitudes of the night and of the sea were present in the cabin. This utter divorce from the varied and protective mechanics of a life ashore. Its complete lack of selectivity. You could not walk down a block and find somebody else. What was on board and who was on board were fixed. Were final. With the only change possible being one of elimination.

It was a small thump, a scratch rather than a knock upon the door.

Another note? Another guiding hand from this ally who preferred the mask of the anonymous? This time Miriam did not wait. She went rapidly over to the door, unbolted it, and flung it open.

Mrs. Vanesse took two careful steps into the cabin.

She looked ghastly. Her fingers clutched a satin dressing gown into a curious knot over her breast. She tottered over to the bed and sank back upon it.

Miriam closed the door. She went swiftly over.

"Are you ill? What has happened, Mrs. Vanesse?"

The woman's voice came with a fearful effort. Moist whisperings after labor. A child's whispering. A child's voice.

"Do not be afraid of me. Put your head down. Here."

The words were accompanied by a smile almost terrific in its angelical grimace, and with her free hand Mrs. Vanesse gently patted the surface of the sheet. The pats were very gentle and then ceased. The other hand relaxed, and it also slipped quietly away from Mrs. Vanesse's breast and lay cupped palm upward at her side. Slowly, released from their hard captivity, the knotted folds in the satin cloth smoothed open and exposed a hilt of a knife. A fleck of carmined froth settled on her lips.

Mrs. Vanesse was dead.

For moments Miriam had no power to move.

Moments of nauseous portent rife with the indecisions of shock. Was she dead? The breast no longer stirred. The eyes were uncovered drops of glass. A tentative finger tip on a flaccid wrist declared no pulse. The hilt of the knife said plainly: It's done. I am the end.

Press the button for Biddle. Call Dr. Crowninshield. Call him. Scream. Shriek yourself into the role of a murderess. Scream out your conversion from schizophrenia into a state of dementia praecox. Call them all in and let them find you in a palsy of hysteria in full view of your bloody deed.

Crowninshield's voice of the afternoon rang in echo: *You must be told the gravity of your state. You must accept the ultimate of its dire importance. Otherwise you would continue to rebel against placing yourself in my hands. Yes, Miss Murcheson, the moment might come when you would even kill.*

The sea.

It was there this body would have to go to seek its burial. At some private moment of the long, dark storm-lashed night. With a flash of panic Miriam bolted the cabin door.

It was she who had been destined for the sea and not that woman over there dead on the bed. Something had slipped. Some cog in this diabolically constructed wheel.

She took a cigarette and struck a match. Her fingers trembled so badly that she could barely light the cigarette. She felt sickeningly weak. The motion of the yacht continued with its incessant pounding as the *Donna Louise* rode into angering seas head on. Miriam sat down in an armchair. She tried to think. She could think nothing but a question that repeated and repeated itself in her head: *What was it that Mrs. Vanesse had really meant to say?*

CHAPTER 16

The sea rose further still under the hour while Miriam sat there, improving its thrusts from the tongues of wind and lifting the *Donna Louise* on each long, strong surge, then leaving her to drop with strengthening shudders of complaint into the trough.

At last, with infinite effort, Miriam stood up. She went into the bathroom and was violently ill. She knelt clinging to marble while hot waves of vicious nausea circled in her head. Then she stood at the basin and slapped cold water on her face. She let the water drip from her skin for a long while, thinking always: I cannot throw that woman into the sea.

Then she thought: Perhaps I will have the strength to carry her back into her cabin. I can leave her there. I must do so. She must not be found with me. Now is the time to try it, while people sleep. Unless the murderer is awake. But he may also be asleep, plunged into dreamless exhaustion from having taken a woman's life.

Was it suicide? Was this the solution Mrs. Vanesse had seized to release herself from the burden that had chained her heart? Was her coming to Miriam's cabin a revulsion of regret at leaving this life, when regret was already too late? Had it been, that coming, a desperate attempt to stumble somewhere and find help?

No. Mrs. Vanesse could have rung for Leclos. She could have pounded on Dr. Crowninshield's door, on Stone's. Miriam's conviction remained that Mrs. Vanesse had had some message to give but that the swiftly closing hand of death had clouded her mind and had caused her to speak those final, meaningless words: "Do not be afraid of me. Put your head down. Here."

Does it matter (Miriam wondered) to me?

It did not. To be found with Mrs. Vanesse's body under any circumstances would convict her of having driven home the knife. It would be she who had killed. She returned to the cabin.

Mrs. Vanesse was heavy, but Miriam called on the strength of desperation to combat the body's flaccid weight. In time, and gauging each motion of the yacht, Mrs. Vanesse was away from the bed and seated on a chair beside the door.

Miriam opened the bolt.

Diagonally across the empty passageway the door to Mrs. Vanesse's cabin swung in arcs, like a fan in casual motion with the boat.

It had best be swiftly done.

Panic gave augmented strength, and after a while they were inside of Mrs. Vanesse's cabin: Miriam and the body of Mrs. Vanesse. The bed had not been slept in. Miriam placed Mrs. Vanesse upon it. She could not leave it sticking there like that, so she covered the handle of the knife with a fold of the dressing gown. There seemed little blood. What there was had been soaked up by the satin folds.

Miriam recalled that woman on the stage who had looked at her hands and had rubbed them together with such great dramatic (if with no practical) effect just after the bloody deed. Miriam observed her own fingers and palms. There was no blood, but there was a stain upon her nightgown. She filed the thought that she must rinse it out.

She pressed shut gently the lids over Mrs. Vanesse's glass-drop eyes.

Tears were present through Miriam's terror, and she knelt for an instant at the bedside in broken prayer. Then she left the cabin and closed its door.

Thinly along the passageway and down from above, through the muffled whine of the wind and sea and the composite groanings of the yacht, came the sound of five bells being struck. Half-past two. The heart and core of the night.

It was odd to be bereft of the power of movement now that the important thing was done, to stand pressed against the wall of the passageway, cowering with a sweat that was beads of ice.

And to think.

First there had been three possible murderers of Jennifer Murcheson to select from, and now there were two: Donald Murcheson and Forsythe Vanesse. Would Forsythe have killed his mother, or was matricide beyond the pale? Would Murcheson have killed his sister? It seemed a less hideous crime. There was a beating terror in it, in standing close-pressed against the wall in the belly of this ship which had horror for its cargo.

Mrs. Vanesse's death must have been suicide. And suicide it must remain.

Miriam freed herself from the magnetic anchorage of the wall and made for her cabin door. It was an unstable journey. She managed to get inside and to swing the door shut when a recurrence of nausea, aided by a soughing rise and shiver of the yacht, hurtled her over to the bed, and she sank upon it. Revulsion at the nature of its recent occupant forced her to leave it at once.

An object of tarnished silver was on the bed table.

It was a swimming blot of darkened silver that steadied into the shape of a locket. Attached to the locket was a brooch pin. The locket was rather large and in the shape of a heart. Miriam picked it up and opened it.

One of its inner sides was bright plain silver. She held the locket by this and attempted to bring into focus a portrait miniature that was inset in the facing side: a young man with a devil-may-care look. A young man of an earlier day. The face started swimming and Miriam closed the locket and dropped it back upon the table.

She struggled to bring some sort of coherence to her thoughts: the locket had not been there when she had left the cabin on her dreadful journey. So someone had come into the cabin and had left it there. For what (again) dark purpose? The murderer, of course. The murderer would have followed, from behind the shelter of some door held infinitesimally ajar, her every move.

Blood.

The stain on her nightgown. She went into the bathroom and rinsed the silk out under a tap with cold water. Red streaked into pink shades. She turned the water off and slid down onto her knees. She lay at length upon the toweling rug.

Her last confused thoughts were on the stupidity of fainting at a moment when something vastly imperative should be attended to. Not the blood. That was taken care of. The bolt. The bolt should be turned to its position where the door would be locked. An effort to rise dribbled out into futility.

Hours later the portholes were gray with a sullen morning's light.

Miriam opened her eyes. She felt stronger and no longer washed about with illness. She stood up and went into the cabin, where she at once bolted the door. Nothing had changed. She looked at her watch. It was nine o'clock. The silk of her nightgown was still damp from where she had rinsed out the blood stain. Her mind worked sharply. She took the nightgown off and dropped it onto the rug near the table. Then she poured milk from the little pitcher over the damp place and let the pitcher lie on it. Biddle would think the pitcher had fallen over during a roll of the ship.

Miriam bathed rapidly and dressed, putting on a warm, fuchsia-colored wool. She corrected the dreary pallor of face with a careful make-up.

She viewed the scene. The scene (Miriam realized) of the crime. There was the bed on which Mrs. Vanesse had died. It looked anything but slept in. She examined its cover carefully for signs of blood. There were none, for Mrs. Vanesse had lain on her back, and the folds of her satin dressing gown had blotted the small amount that had trickled from the wound. Miriam did her best to make the bed look slept in, rumpling the covers and the pillows.

The sea had not abated, and there was a screaming note in the echo of the wind.

Something had changed.

Miriam looked for it, but could not find it: the tarnished silver locket holding the miniature of the devil-may-care young man. Its importance grew in her mind. It became increasingly the crux of this situation in which she had been trapped. The very casualness of the locket's coming and going cried its significance to be the reverse.

Mrs. Vanesse and her lifelong girlhood friend Edna (this thought was coming back) who had stolen (*yes*) a heart-shaped silver locket from a mutual friend, a Beatrice Shaftsbury, aged six. And while Mrs. Vanesse had been recounting it, the anecdote had seemed but a surface representation of some inner meaning which its words had been meant to convey. Had Mrs. Vanesse brought the locket in with her and dropped it on the table before collapsing on the bed?

Miriam looked, as a last resort, in her handbag. The locket was not there.

She left the cabin and went up on deck.

CHAPTER 17

Miriam went into the dining saloon. She felt that she must do this, must keep all of her actions as normal as possible, must blot out from her mind any knowledge of what had happened below.

Forsythe was in the middle of kidneys. He was not alone. Murcheson and Stone were also breakfasting. They stood up and greeted her, and Murcheson seated her at his right. There was nothing remotely murderous about any of them. Each had a fresh-as-a-daisy look.

"I'm afraid we are in for it," Murcheson said. "Captain Liggett tells me there will be a blow. Storm warnings are up along this entire stretch of coast. Fortunately our course will cut across its path at a favorable angle. I know nothing about seamanship whatever, but the captain seems to derive some comfort from that fact. They caught it in New Jersey."

Forsythe said, "The 'it' referred to is a minor hurricane with a half-mile-wide path. The property damage amounts to millions, the toll in lives but six. Would you call it a commentary on our times that the money loss always receives preferential spacing in the press?" He speared a kidney and added, "Rather a far remove from the nothing of a single sparrow's fall."

"You are not," Stone said, "acquainted with the personal habits of sparrows."

"I am not. But whatever they are I'm against their extermination, which is what I suppose you are indirectly suggesting. I am a believer in freedom of habits. A point which Roosevelt and Churchill missed during their conference at sea. Aren't we slipping far afield?" He glanced rather long at Miriam and said, "How did you sleep?"

"Very well, thank you."

"The motion failed to bother you?"

"No, I am getting accustomed to it." She looked up at Branch, who stood waiting for her order. "Simply coffee and toast, please. And orange juice."

How stupid to believe, Miriam thought, that you could penetrate a person's mind. No mask was so perfect as the human face itself. Where did you find it? What form of manifestation did it take: the mark of Cain?

Then tremulous but unmistakable, and muted by the distance from its source, which was the deck below, came the sound of a woman screaming. It froze them into the momentary bewilderment of shock. Miriam knew. And perhaps one other among them knew it too: that Mrs. Vanesse's body had been found.

Miriam looked neither at Forsythe nor at Murcheson in any attempt to read in their expressions some label of guilt. She looked at Stone, at a dawning horror settling in his eyes as he stared directly back at her. She wanted to cry out to him: No. I have done nothing. I have not killed.

The spell broke, and all of them were moving out of the saloon and toward the source of the scream with that reserved haste so curiously thought good form by people of intelligence when faced with an uncharted disaster. The let-there-be-no-panic brake on speed and a hint of the national anthem hanging unsung about them in the air.

Leclos was recovered from her shock when they reached her in Mrs. Vanesse's cabin. She stood pale and shaken, flanked by Biddle and the deck steward, Murray.

The familiar shape of death did not stun Stone into immobility at the doorway. Crashing into his heart came the belief that Crowninshield had, after all, been right. This girl, this lovely thing (all of whose aspects both inside and out were so warm and so beautiful) was not only a schizophrene but had slipped further across the border line into the sickening morasses of homicidal mania.

Had she been driven there by him? By his badgering doubts which now seemed so puerile whereas, in contrast, how sound, how titanic loomed Crowninshield's brain. If this were true, then he and not she was the murderer. And where was it to end? He glanced covertly at Miriam. Her face was innocent of the shocked surprise and horror which would be normal unless she were already aware that Mrs. Vanesse had been killed. A rush of shame and desire swept through him to help her. To cure her. To shelter her from any further act against some other person or (he felt sharp fright) against herself.

Murcheson, following one incredulous and agonized look toward the body on the bed, cried out, "Stone—don't stand there. Do something."

Stone managed to get a grip upon himself.

"We are hours too late for that, Mr. Murcheson."

"Make sure. You can't tell from over there. Kate can't be dead."

Leclos was making low noises which Miriam had always associated in her imagination with what keening must be like.

Forsythe turned on Leclos sharply and said, "Stop it!"

"I am sorry. I am not in command of my emotions. It is I who have found her. Regard! I enter. Madam does not move. She does not breathe. I lift the folds of Madam's gown and behold the hilt of the knife."

"You what?" Stone asked.

"I behold the knife."

"Didn't you say that you lifted the folds of the gown?"

"Yes."

Stone went to the bed. His hands were busy for a while in the stillness that formed a small nugget in the ship's mass of sound, its endless laboring creaks, the rip of water along the outer shell, the angered noise of wind through the rigging up above.

"I would say," Stone said, "that your sister died somewhere between midnight and three this morning, Mr. Murcheson. That is the best I can give you on snap judgment."

"What earthly difference does it make?" Murcheson asked. "Why did she do it? Why did Kate kill herself?"

"You consider it suicide?"

"That is unhappily obvious. Don't you?"

Stones face was pale. Here was an out for her. And for him. Let it go. Let it rest as suicide. Abnegate all oaths and the moral structure of the years. He looked at her again. She was stricken enough all right now. Sick with it. Wondering what he would say. Suppose she hadn't done it? He had been wrong once. This conflict gave his voice the remarkable effect of a stuffed shirt delivering a lecture.

"I have found this about suicides, Mr. Murcheson. My conclusions are drawn from two years of experience on the medical examiners' corps. Rarely does a woman use a knife. For murder, yes. For suicide, no. There is an abhorrence about it inherent in the female make-up. Further, an initial success at achieving death with a knife is most rare. This wound is a clean, lethal plunge. I would have expected the more tentative and ineffective first attempts to accompany it. I do not deny that it could be suicide. I simply state that if it is so, the case is unique. Certainly it is to me." Murcheson turned to Murray.

"We must put in at once. Request Captain Liggett to join us, please."

"Yes, sir."

Murray left, and Murcheson walked over to Miriam.

He said, "Your own sad problem must not be lost sight of in the natural bewilderment of our grief. I cannot understand it. I can think of nothing, of no reason on earth why Kate should have done this." He appealed to Forsythe. "Surely her life was happy? You have been with her more constantly throughout the last years than I have. Was there some secret illness? Some trouble that preyed upon her mind? I had noticed no sign of there being one."

"Mother never complained."

"But you felt something? You sensed that something was there?"

"It is so easy to say yes when you think back. Things begin to assume importance after an event has occurred." Stone turned from the body. He said, "I shall ask you to be witnesses to the fact that the eyes are closed." He looked at Leclos. "Did you close them?"

"No, Doctor. Everything is as I found Madam. I approached. I saw. I retreated in horror, to find that I had screamed."

"Everything is not as you found her. You removed the folds of the dressing gown from the hilt of the knife."

"That, yes. That only. No more."

"What about Kate's eyes?" Murcheson asked.

"They would be open if someone had not closed their lids," Stone said. "I also contend that the hilt of the knife would be exposed if Mrs. Vanesse had driven the blade in herself."

Murcheson revolved the implications gloomily. With slow deliberation his look settled on Miriam and stayed there. His face became expressive with a dawning horror. He erased the look at once.

He said, "It is folly ever to jump to conclusions. It is the most foolish thing I know of. There can be a thousand reasons why a tree should fall." He placed his hands gently upon Miriam's shoulders. "I do not have much confidence in your powers to resist the shock of this. Go with Biddle, my dear. You can be of no service here. Remove yourself from this tragedy and try, if you can, to erase it from your thoughts."

"That would be impossible, Mr. Murcheson."

"Perhaps you are right. But at least go above to the main saloon. Biddle will stay there with you. Later we will join you."

Murcheson smiled at her in the kindliest and most concerned fashion. It was not just a passing or a conventional gesture. It was as though her immediate welfare were paramount to his own grief and the horror inherent in a questioned death. Miriam felt as though he were putting her in a balance but had already tipped the scale a favorable minim on her side.

The obverse interpretation could however be acceptable: that *had* he killed his sister an insistence on a swift verdict of suicide would be overwhelmingly essential to his own security, and would be far preferable to the task of proving hers to be the guilty hand.

Miriam would have preferred to stay and to follow, at no matter what detriment to her own interests, Stone's further probing into details as damning as the shutting of Mrs. Vanesse's eyes. It was a curious paradox for the feeling still to persist: that her safety continued to rest with Stone even though there might lie in his expert knowledge of criminology a not improbable legal extinction of her life on the charge of murder. She loved him.

That was the truth of her thinking all this. The undoubted abhorrence of his thoughts concerning her were no deterrent, no brake on this love which had taken possession of her. Murderess. Love was a word which Miriam faintly disliked. It had been too bandied about, with careless usage, too overcloyed with the mawkishness of crooning baritones and sick-cat contraltos, and still there was no other. Take it or leave it, with its sainted rhymes of doves and aboves.

As Miriam left the cabin she heard Murcheson say, "We must look for a suicide note. I am positive that Kate would never have done such a ghastly thing as this without leaving some explanation as to why."

CHAPTER 18

Miriam went with Biddle in a mental meekness which persisted until Captain Liggett encountered them at the head of the stairway. Liggett was carrying the storm clouds down with him from the bridge. An outraged annoyance lined his face that this gratuitous worry of a tragedy dealing in merely human elements should intrude itself within his rightful field of care, the security of his ship, which he knew to be riding into weather unpredictably hazardous. His good sound Methodist core compelled him to pause for the amenities no matter how sharp his irritation at the source which held them called for.

"My sympathies, Miss Lake, at this unhappy blow."

"Thank you, Captain Liggett."

"May you find comfort in the good word."

"Thank you."

(One final embellishment and the job would be done.)

"In the midst of life we are in death."

Period. And Liggett was off, hurrying down the steps.

"He is deeply religious," Biddle said as they went on into the saloon. "Most captains are, I've found. It usually hits them when they get their first command. I suppose it's having nobody over them to rely on or to pass the buck to. Nobody but God. I'm not being sacrilegious. It just happens to be so. Let's sit down over here and talk, Miss Lake. It will do you good."

Miriam sat and looked incuriously at Biddle. Then her interest sharpened as she wondered what the change was in the woman. The henna dye was still vivid on Biddle's hair, and the small lines graven in her face were neither more nor less prominent in this gray light of the storm-cast day. Biddle still had the skinny look. It was her eyes. There was a flutter about them, a certain calculating look which was at variance with the random tenor of her chatter.

"I've never put much stock in specialists," Biddle went on. "Sometimes it seems they just can't help being too smart for their own good. I'm thinking of Dr. Stone."

"I gathered that you were."

"He'll do his best to make a murder out of this just because a couple of details don't gibe with the cases he's run into before. He doesn't know what he's up against. He's in a different world than the one he's used to, out here on the high seas."

"Why should it be different?"

"Well, the captain is the police department, the district attorney's office, and the medical examiners' corps all rolled into one. That is, when there isn't any real question of doubt. I don't mean in an instance where the murderer would be actually caught red-handed." Biddle fluttered her eyes and then added, "Or where it could be made obvious that the case *was* one of murder and the guilt of some *definite person* could be practically established. Then the thing would have to follow the usual course."

"What is the usual course?"

"Oh, the person would be arraigned before a United States Commissioner in United States District Court at the first port of call. I imagine that the captain will put in for Newport News or Baltimore, incidentally. That's where the case would be prosecuted, too. Then if the person is convicted and sentenced to be hanged, the place of hanging is determined by the Attorney General." (The eyes fluttered extravagantly.) "The Federal government doesn't electrocute in such cases, Miss Lake. It hangs."

"You seem to have gone into it."

"I was on the *Garfield* back in thirty-four when they had a stabbing during a drinking bout. A couple of the passengers. The case came up and a jury brought in a verdict of not guilty in twenty-seven minutes. Even so it couldn't have been a pleasant thing to have to face, a trial for murder."

"Certainly not pleasant."

"No, and that's why I hope Dr. Stone doesn't get too bitten by this sleuthing bug and go rooting out a lot of testimony that possibly has no bearing on the case at all."

"Testimony?"

"You know the way people talk, the way they speculate about things. Personally, I always try to keep my mouth shut. I guess I'm selfish. I try to figure out how things will be best for me."

"Best in what way?"

"You can understand this, Miss Lake, because you're a woman. Most of my life I've worked for rich people, on luxury liners, on yachts, and I've had tastes of luxury myself while on shore leaves. Or I've kidded myself into believing that I had. But there's always been a sailing day to cut them short, and I'm back in harness again."

Biddle sat a little straighter, a little more tensely in the chair. Her voice took on an edge.

"I used to dream about a break coming along," she went on. "I used to dream that some rich old ape on the passenger list would fall for me. That was during the early days, when people said I reminded them of Gloria Swanson, instead of thinking that I look like the Flying Dutchman as they do now. She's that wreck that shoves her bones around in the Sargasso Sea."

"Yes, but there is no comparison."

"Miss Lake, I don't kid myself. I'm through. My success in a water-front tavern is limited to some windy old crock awash in a barrel of rum. That's my present tops. So that's why I try to figure out how things will be best for me."

"Yes, I can understand that, but I don't see how it applies in this instance."

Biddle's bone-thin fingers were trembling. The bracelet of pressed butterfly wings was a nervous ripple of emerald fire.

"I could do with a drink. I could do with a good double hooker of rye right now. But I never drink on duty. It dulls my mind. It loosens my tongue. I grow less acute to little details which are part of my job."

"Wouldn't it be simpler if you came to the point?"

"Oh, don't think that. There isn't any *point*. I'd never dream of forcing anything to a point, Miss Lake, no matter how much it would be to my advantage."

"You've repeated that phrase several times. I wish you would explain it."

I don't (Miriam thought); I don't wish it at all. She has connected something in my cabin with the fact that Mrs. Vanesse died there. It's obviously her first attempt to blackmail. She's onto something but she's afraid of being too blunt about it.

Miriam found herself feeling curiously sorry for Biddle. Surely this loomed for Biddle as her one great chance, amazingly dropped by fate into her lap at the turn of life when all hope for the breaks was gone. Heaven knew what fields of luxury were opened up for Biddle to plunder in, for her assurance surely lay in the conviction that she, Miriam, was a woman of wealth, and nothing that Miriam could say would disillusion her. So there Biddle was, holding over Miriam the possible power of life or death. How much to ask? How much to make Miriam pay? Miriam saw all these things while she watched the determination hardening the lines in Biddle's face.

"My work, Miss Lake, has resolved around beds. I know all about them. I've seen and fixed up so many beds that I can tell how they've been slept in and how the sleeper slept. As for spotting that a bed hasn't been slept in, that's a cinch. I mean where any attempt has been made to make it seem as though it had been."

(Better fight this now.)

"Then you noticed that I failed to sleep in mine last night?"

"Yes. You couldn't miss that."

"I was ill."

"I know."

"I sat up in a chair. I only lay down on the bed for a moment toward morning."

"You don't use silver hairpins, Miss Lake."

"Of course I don't."

Biddle's fingers were suddenly quiet.

"Mrs. Vanesse did."

So there it was. One of Mrs. Vanesse's hairpins had dropped in the bed. It was perhaps one of several little things from which the truth could be reconstructed with absurd facility by Stone. It would be Biddle's word against her own, but one word from Biddle would be appalling. It would force suspicion over into the realm of conviction.

Always, over every other consideration was the unshakable belief on the part of competent authority (Dr. Crowninshield) of her schizophrenic condition and of her identity as Jennifer Murcheson. And of Dr. Crowninshield's belief that under the proper compulsion she might kill.

Biddle was saying, "Funny about that milk upsetting on your nightgown, Miss Lake. I took the nightgown. Ill take care of it."

"My hand struck the pitcher during a roll."

Biddle looked at her pityingly.

"The milk stain will come out all right. Milk's not like some things. Say like blood. It's terribly hard to wash out blood. They've chemical tests or something that will show the smallest trace of it." Biddle's hands resumed their trembling. Her eyes were shifty. "The wind is getting stronger, Miss Lake."

"Considerably stronger."

"It's the miserable days like this one which make me discontented with a life at sea. It makes me feel I'd do a lot if somebody would be kind and generous and make it possible for me to live a happy life ashore. I'd be grateful, Miss Lake. I'd be grateful in a very practical way."

Biddle started to shiver all over under the compulsion of this act which was so at variance with the hearty kindliness of her entire existence, an existence which had been (no matter how automatically so) one of ministration to the wants of others. It was possible that she would have turned and would have revoked her entire intention if Murray had not come into the saloon and said that Dr. Crowninshield would be most happy if Miss Lake would be kind enough to join him in the library.

Biddle stood up, too.

She said to Miriam, "Later."

CHAPTER 19

Crowninshield remained seated. He apologized for not arising and mentioned his knees, the maladroit state of which had further been aggravated by the increasing motion of the vessel. He waved Miriam into a near-by armchair with delicately beautiful fingers (it was his private impression that they were on a par with those of Stokowski) and completed the gesture with a stroke or two bestowed upon his silken beard.

"Miss Murcheson, it is my happy privilege to tell you that there no longer remains even the vestige of a doubt. That is, as to your true identity. You are Jennifer Murcheson. It has been proved."

"In what manner, Doctor?"

"By Dr. Stone. It is not that any real doubt formerly existed, but the evidence which has just been found is of a nature that would stand without contradiction from opposing experts in any court of law. I refer to your fingerprints."

"Doctor, this is the final absurdity. My fingerprints are the one thing that will prove me to be myself, Miriam Lake." Pink lips smiled.

"As a scientist I am averse to extrasensory phenomena, but there have been moments when even I was impressed by that *déclassé* but remarkable business known as chance. Such a moment has but recently occurred. Within the hour. There are certain attributes which appertain to a suicidal death."

"Are you then satisfied, Doctor, that Mrs. Vanesse did take her own life?"

"Yes. Completely satisfied. Stone remains in doubt. I suspect him of being in the clutches of an emotional upset quite extraneous to the problem of Mrs. Vanesse's death. I shall defer being more definite and simply attribute his confusions to the fact that doubt is a habit of the young. It forms as essential a part of their daily nourishment as bread and meat. I am tolerant. I would not have him betray his years."

"I should scarcely call him a youngster."

"Twenty-six? My dear Miss Murcheson, from my pinnacle in the eighties! There is scarcely more than a scratch upon the record of his life."

"With only a dot, I suppose, on mine."

"A dot. You put it very well. Both of you are buds with life tight within you, dark, tightly pressed petals that need opening by the sun. Only the years can unfurl them."

He'll go on like this (Miriam thought) until he has wrung the last pistil dry. Crowninshield did. He pursued a self-enchanted pathway from epicalyx (the tots) through calyx (the teens) and the several intermediate unfurlings, all of which terminated at the gynoecium, and himself as a very full-blown rose, one of a most intellectual specie complete with beard.

He returned to Stone.

"Stone's dip into legal medicine while attached to the medical examiners' corps did not fail to imbue him with a spicy interest in crime detection as a hobby. Propinquity, of course, with the visible specimens of so many unnatural deaths and a touch of the human-emotional brushes that had tarred them and vicariously himself. There is a word called kibitzing."

"I know it."

"Really? I found it abstruse until it was explained to me. Now I relish it for its tang. He kibitzed."

"Dr. Stone?"

"Yes. He did it among the various departments of criminal investigation. In some he became modestly proficient, and among the whorls and loops of fingerprint patterns remarkably so. He has identified yours as being identical with those of Jennifer Murcheson. I am tremendously gratified, because up until now your identification has rested primarily upon handwriting. There have been too many opposing opinions given out by experts in calligraphy to my liking."

"Is there anything more commonplace than forgery, Doctor?"

"I will admit that the point had cast a slender shadow across my mind. It has been effaced. My dear girl, you *are you*."

"I know it. I have been saying it. I still say it."

"No, be calm. I must insist. I return to your aunt's suicide. One of the attributes to have been expected was a suicide note, that ultimate rebellion of the human spirit against not being understood. That final, defensive, explanatory word which must be left before their irremediable plunge through death's dark curtains. A pathetic link. A wishful anchor left. We searched among Mrs. Vanesse's effects for such a note. There was none. But there was a locket."

"Silver and heart-shaped?"

The words escaped before Miriam could check them. Crowninshield gave a small cry of triumph and stood up excitedly, in spite of his knees.

He took several steps that were (somewhat impeded by the rolling of the yacht) a conqueror's strut.

"You are coming through. Your true self is coming through. You remember the locket."

Yes, Miriam remembered the locket. She would never forget it. And what was left her? She could say this: I carried Mrs. Vanesse's freshly dead body from my cabin to her cabin so that I would not be accused of having murdered her. When I returned someone had placed that locket on my bed table. I opened it, and that is how my fingerprints happen to be on the smooth inside surface. I fainted. When I came to, the locket had been taken away. In other words, I am the complete fool.

She was cooked.

Crowninshield was going on his soaring enthusiasm lending a chirruping effect to his didactic voice.

"You are bridging back across the years. That locket, my dear, my happy girl, was taken by Mrs. Vanesse from the dressing table of your room in the ranch in California on the day of your father's funeral. That was *six years ago*. Since that moment it has been constantly in Mrs. Vanesse's possession, a cherished, stolen memento of her brother. And here is where the astoundingly important psychological point comes in."

"Surely, Doctor, she would have opened it frequently to look at the miniature? That would have effaced old fingerprints."

A second cry of delight issued from pink lips.

"Good! The fact that the locket contains a miniature has come through."

Miriam plowed on.

"I insist that her fingerprints would have erased any left by Jennifer Murcheson six years ago."

"Cease—I must beg of you—do not let this Miriam Lake fight on. No one opened that locket again after Mrs. Vanesse stole it from the dresser. No one disturbed the prints that had been left in it by its owner, Jennifer Murcheson. You."

"That would be impossible to prove, Doctor."

"We have the proof. It concerns the psychological point I spoke of. Your aunt held a strongly antagonistic feeling for your father. That was undoubtedly because of his own antipathy toward herself, her mode of living, and the way in which she was bringing up her son. She did not care to look upon your father's face again."

"Then why did she take the locket?"

"She took it because her childhood affection for him was so deeply rooted in her subconscious that, even though he were dead, it could not cast this affection loose. She knew that his miniature was in the locket. In spite of her conscious dislike for your father, her subconscious longing forced her to keep the locket always with her, unopened, unlooked upon, as hidden fodder for this hidden love. Surely you must see?"

"You are again adjusting your imagination to suit your theories."

"I adjust nothing. The locket was found by us in a plain, sealed envelope. It was folded in a letter which briefly outlined in layman's language the facts I have just advanced. It was simple for me to amplify, to read between the lines. I may say in passing that Doctor Stone agrees in toto." Crowninshield gestured negligently. "A tyro among my former students could have done as well."

The moment held a Scylla-and-Charybdian leer.

If Miriam proved the fingerprints in the locket were placed there by her last night, it still would not disprove her to be Jennifer Murcheson. It would just convince this bedazzled old goat that Jennifer Murcheson had slipped from the schizophrenic into the paranoic or the manic-depressive and had killed Mrs. Vanesse. Possibly because (in her mad state) she had just discovered Mrs. Vanesse's theft of the locket with its miniature of her adored father.

Surely a true fingerprint of Jennifer Murcheson must exist somewhere among her effects or about the ranch house in California? Such prints could be identifiably transmitted by radio, or certainly their precise classification could be. If Miriam's were of a different classification, it would at least free her from this lethal incubus of a double identity. It would spike the murderer's plot to kill her. But that would take time.

There was no time.

Surely tonight (as they were to head for the nearest port) the murderer would have to arrange that she vanish at sea. The locket would be introduced in court to establish her identity, to be her corpus delicti, and Jennifer Murcheson would be accidentally dead. Having presumably taken her own life during a deranged period of the process of sticking her split personality together again. Dr. Crowninshield's technical blow-by-blow summation of this process would undoubtedly be, well, succulent.

On the other hand, if she did not prove the locket print was that of Miriam Lake's, it was all over with her but for the dirge. A wedge of doubt could be attempted. He (goat) expected this Miriam Lake half to fight to the last breath.

"Doctor, why is it only now that the question of fingerprints has come up? What was the name of that agency? The one which conducted the search for Jennifer Murcheson?"

"The Durney people, and I see the point you are driving at. Your Miriam Lake still fights. You will ask me why the Durney people did not establish a sample of your fingerprints from some personal belonging of yours at the ranch. Two facts intervened. The time element, and the excellent control you held over your servants as a chatelaine."

"They had cleaned the place?"

"Polished, washed, scoured, and scrubbed. Have I missed anything?"

"Dusted."

"Dusted. Furthermore, they knew you as a creature of strong, impulsive will. Several days passed before they dared to presume even a wonder about your absence. You had ridden away. When it pleased you, you would return. At last a search was undertaken of your numberless acres for your remains. It was a difficult affair because they were satisfied in their simple fashion that you were occupied with some willful impulse of the moment. A full week went by before your major domo—you now remember Matanza?"

"I do not."

"Then I shall assist your subconscious. Matanza is a Mexican who possesses both ability and intelligence to a high degree, but during his years in your service you have imbued him with an acceptance of your word as law. Your movements, your impulses were never to be questioned. You killed his initiative. That is why he waited a full week before daring to wire for instructions from your uncle. Your uncle replied that he would fly west immediately. This threw your staff into a greater furor of scouring, with the result that the darkest corner and your least possession were polished pins."

"Are my prints on the outside of that locket also, Doctor?"

Crowninshield gave a disappointed cluck.

"Surely your mind is too keen for that. We naturally handled it after it was removed from the envelope. Fortunately none of us opened it before the note had been read, and Stone was then instantly aware of the tremendous importance of the chance that a print of yours might be on its inside. There was. Stone checked it with one on a glass in your bathroom. I gasp at the thought that we might have destroyed it."

"I gasp at his brilliance, Doctor. He has signed my death warrant."

Crowninshield had no intention of missing this one. If he felt that his fingers were artistically comparable to Stokowski's, he was certain that his ability to turn a phrase was as neat as a Talleyrand's.

"The death warrant of Miriam Lake, my dear. But he has signed a birth certificate, too. For Jennifer Murcheson is reborn."

A shattering sea caught the *Donna Louise* on her quarter and hurtled Crowninshield with thistledown agility into Miriam's lap.

CHAPTER 20

Macabre was the word for the sky, Miriam thought, after she had disentangled Crowninshield and had gone out on deck. She stood at the rail and gripped a stanchion while spume carried on the wind's whine whipped her cheeks. She considered the funereal coloration of the sky and sea; somber, sullen grays with white satin trim: a fluid coffin slowly going Dali. It would be worse during the darkness of the night, when her screams would be dismissed as mere tremolos added to the storm.

Forsythe interrupted her wretched thoughts. He joined her at the rail, with *plage*-tanned hands gripping it strongly, and there was suddenly something likable about him. This was perhaps because Miriam felt a genuine reaction of a real liking in him for her. You could tell that. When a person was truly interested in you. Truly liked you.

It removed him with abruptness from his role of a suspected murderer in Miriam's private reading of the plot. He could have killed, as any of us under a given set of circumstances might kill, but he could never have killed his mother. Every instinct in Miriam convinced her of it. He was not smiling. He was no longer gay. He was, in this serious repose, an extremely personable man.

"It is to be Baltimore," he said.

"We're putting in?"

"Yes. The course is already changed. You probably felt it when we caught it on the beam."

"I felt it and Dr. Crowninshield. When will we land?"

"Some time tomorrow. It is according to how much the weather slows us during the night. We're logging around fifteen knots now."

Some time tomorrow. So the time limit was set. The balance of the daylight seemed improbable for an attack, but after dusk should fall and night close in, then during its long black hours the attempt upon her life would have to be made if it were to be made at all.

The *Donna Louise* would drop anchor with the body of Mrs. Vanesse lying in state. Her niece would be listed as missing. Overboard during the night. The locket with its fingerprint and its documentary verification, her corresponding fingerprint from the bathroom glass, both would be offered in probate as the corpus delicti. The murderer could pen *finis* on the happy ending of his scheme.

Forsythe said, "Dr. Crowninshield has told you, of course?"

"About the locket? Yes."

"It is the only happy feature about my mother's death. I am sorry about her death for many reasons. For one thing we were very close. We were used to each other. I suppose by that I mean there was little of the petty friction which usually accompanies consistently intimate relationships. We enjoyed the same things. We were satisfied with the same manner of life. That manner which your father considered to be detrimentally frivolous."

"Miss Murcheson's father."

"Very well. Your clinging to being this Miriam Lake is another reason why my mother's death is upsetting. It is a tragic interruption of your cure. With weeks, with months of leisure before us as we had planned it, with your present self divorced from that false world it had created, Dr. Crowninshield assured us that he could bring you back again. The real you."

Forsythe observed her gravely for a moment before going on. His face was more infernally handsome than ever because of this grave concern.

He said, "Frankly, now I am worried. I am not a fool. None of us is. Dr. Stone continues to balk at a plain verdict, of suicide. He clings to some fantastic notion that Mother was murdered, although he refuses to make any open accusation. But he has told us flatly that when we reach Baltimore he will insist upon an official investigation of some sort. I am afraid that you will leave us during that time while we are held up there. There will be many avenues for escape. On board, if our voyage had gone on, there would have been none."

Leclos's words came back to Miriam in the stewardess's interpretation of Forsythe's character: He has many faces. Each has the facet of a well-cut gem and is pleasant to look upon. I can offer no proper précis of young Mr. Vanesse. Miriam said, "Will you tell me the time, please?" Forsythe looked at his watch.

"Half-past ten."

Monday morning, and the offices of the Powers agency and the *Bazaar* were open. It was stupid to ignore that final chance. But was she checkmated even in this? Was Biddle's testimony of the hairpin, the unslept-in bed, the possible remnants of a bloodstain on the nightgown enough to involve her in a murder charge? Plenty. Nevertheless, if it were proved she were Miriam Lake to Crowninshield's satisfaction, any question of schizophrenia with subsequent murderous manias would be dissolved, and her story of the night and of the locket would stand a far better chance of carrying conviction. For what earthly motive would Miriam Lake have for murdering Mrs. Vanesse?

Most essential of all, however, once she was established as herself, as Miriam Lake, she would be sheltered from the murderer's attack. Her death would cease to have any value to him. No motive would be left him but pique at a plot gone wrong.

"I want to send two wireless messages," she said.

"I'm afraid they will have to wait awhile."

"Why?"

"Simmonds is ill."

Yes, and that was simple too, as the locket business had been simple. Nothing so gauche as damage done to the wireless set. No refusal to permit her to send rational messages which were so vital to the presentation of her case. Simply no operator. There must have been illimitable choices of a drug which, slipped into his midnight lunch, would keep Simmonds ill for as long as would be required.

"Is he seriously ill?"

"Dr. Crowninshield is puzzled. He has fever and a touch of delirium. Leclos has been assigned to nurse him. Crowninshield decided on a sedative. The boy is the nervous type. May I ask the nature of the messages?"

"It doesn't matter. They're of no consequence now."

"You seem rather gloomy about them."

"I am."

"Funny."

"There is nothing funny about it."

"I don't mean the messages. I mean it's funny about you. The way you've changed. Six years ago, if anything had balked you, you would have flown into a screaming rage. I can assure you from personal memories that you were the perfect hellcat."

"There's no earthly use in going on with this."

"Yes there is. Even your face has developed. You were attractive enough in a way, but now you're blazing. You have that cigarette-ad glow. All you need is a background of two dazed sailors stricken dumber than usual with admiration."

This could not be so. But it was so. It was there all right: the moist, calf look. A speculative birth of desire. It was an outrageous thing to appear so closely on the heels of violent death. An affront against decency and nature. Miriam considered how objectionable the swift arising of a passion could be if it came from an undesired source. With Stone it would have been so different. Even a damp look, much less a moist-calf one, would have rung a bell.

Leclos on Forsythe came back in more detail: Mr. Forsythe Vanesse is possessed of that wit and that facile charm only natural to such a birth and the cosmopolitan milieu of his upbringing.

Maybe so. Perhaps it was properly *de rigueur* in continental circles for moisture to shift so facilely from dolor to desire. My maternal love is dead, long live my love for cigarette-ad faces. Grim. She glanced again at Forsythe. His eyes had popped back in a little. That was good.

He said, "You're very intuitive. You've realized that *I've* realized that you've suddenly become a person. Very strongly one. You are also affronted at this untimeliness. Why? Such things from their very nature are unpredictable and therefore beyond control. Any of the other emotions can be aroused by design. You can make people laugh or cry or fear. It is done every day in the theater and in books. But you cannot make them feel love. That comes of its own accord and whenever it will."

Was it a line? Miriam thought not. Was it some attack which he had tested and found true beneath a series of tropical moons? No. It was genuine. It was novel to him, too. Miriam doubted whether there had ever been a stranger avowal or one made under circumstances more inappropriate than these.

What, could you do? Smile sadly and fade gently away? Not unless you were adroit at abracadabra. You could not say: Look here, my lad, your mother is just dead. This spot you're trying to turn into a tryst is a floating tomb. Shakespeare could have knocked a better job together. Something on the line of: Go get thee to thy breviary, Coz. Then stage directions which would include the wave of a cross and an exit upper left.

"Don't you think," she said, "that we had better drop this?"

"Yes. That would be best." His sudden grin was at its most enchanting. "At least for now."

CHAPTER 21

The day passed slowly with the lethargy of a heavy dream, a pace which was in contrast with the sullen violence of the ever mounting sea. Deadlights were fastened on the ports, and everything movable made fast. Mrs. Vanesse was made fast, too, with sheets that bound her to the bed, their mechanism hidden by a coverlet of rose-toned silk.

Crowninshield and Stone were closeted for several hours with Murcheson after lunch. This had offered Miriam the choice between penning herself up in her cabin, which meant solitary confinement with her drearily lethal thoughts, or a continuation of propinquity with Forsythe, who hovered about her and offered for her amusement each one in turn of his numerous faces. Their variant masks had swung with intermediate steps between a grief-ridden son to (again) a swain whose passions were trembling on the boil.

There had been one further brush with Biddle.

It occurred in the passageway when Miriam had gone below following lunch for a moment in her cabin.

"Miss Murcheson—"

(It seemed that orders had been issued by Crowninshield since the fingerprint-locket episode that she was to be addressed as Miss Murcheson and no longer as Miss Lake. Evidently Miss Lake was to be officially dead. A dress rehearsal of that moment in the coming night when the storm-tossed waters would receive her, and Miss Murcheson also would have officially died.)

"Yes, Biddle?"

"Have you thought?"

"About an appropriate payment for your blackmail?" The woman was wretched: a sparse aging rip on the rack, still torn between her innate goodliness and this gripping chance of a down-filled bed in which to coddle her no longer attractive bones. A final golden whirl among the fleshpots and the vintaged fruits of the vine.

"Don't say that," Biddle said. "Don't think of me as a blackmailer. Think of me as an ally, as a friend."

"Don't be absurd.'

"I'm not. Maybe friend isn't the right word. Accessory after the fact, you could call it. The thing is this. You've got plenty. You'd never miss it. Just a thin slice of what you've got—"

Biddle's eyes were suddenly overflowing with tears. Her lower lashes dripped mascara.

She went on: "It would mean such a terrible, such a hell of a lot to me, Miss Murcheson. You don't know what it's like to feel that your life is coming to its close in the same deadly manner in which you've always lived it—pots, and vomit, and sheets, and rich old women bullying you for 'specials' and being suspicious like a pack of thwarted weasels that you haven't brought them the 'best.' I'm sick of that look. I've seen it again and again, their eyes like lances, sometimes only on a strip of bacon. That's how it is, Miss Murcheson. That's *why*."

"Biddle, will you believe this? I have no money. I am not Miss Murcheson. I'm a woman of no earthly importance by the name of Miriam Lake. I would give you your slice if I had it and if I were that Murcheson girl."

Biddle wiped her eyes. She shrugged thin shoulders. Her voice shifted into a thick malevolence.

"We're due in Baltimore tomorrow, Miss Murcheson. The authorities will board the boat. Dr. Stone is going to insist that they investigate. I will give you until then."

The ensuing three hours were passed with Forsythe and his chameleon changes, while the ship's bells were assuming for Miriam the quality of a somber processional marking with slow-paced chronometrical steps the march toward night.

Throughout the three hours Forsythe offered in much detail a self-portrait brushed in many schools which ranged from the academic to surrealism stripped to its most Freudian images of dislocated dreams. The child, the youth, the man. An endless succession of scamperings over the globe, with rest notes furnished by the better-known casinos, beaches, and spas.

That sort of thing, Forsythe said, entered your blood stream like a virus. You could not any longer light. It cut out of your system the sedentary and the ability to sink some roots into a patch of ground and (there) to grow. The world's honey could be sipped but never nurtured in a hive. Did you nurture honey? No. Well then, but Jennifer would know what he meant.

Of course it made for peccadilloes, "having affairs," as some people called it, those who were addicts of euphuism. It made you scared. It frightened you into wondering whether you were any longer capable of recognizing the real thing when you met it. The lasting thing. Done with bonk and bell and candle and St. Thomas' doorsteps gritty with rice.

So there you were. A waif both physically and of the soul. And that, according to Forsythe, was Forsythe. Right then he would say no more. He would let the delicate harpoons of what he had said sink. Either to fester or (as he so obviously at the moment considered desirable) to flip her gently into his net.

The emergence of Murcheson and Crowninshield and Stone from their conference in the library came as a release. They lingered in the main saloon for highballs brought by Murray.

Murcheson cut Miriam loose from Forsythe and herded her onto a Knole sofa sheened with lemon-colored damask. He sat rather close in a comfortable intimacy, as though no further reason existed why he should not do so. An uncle and his niece. An odor of Russian leather sifted dimly from his clothes and hair. In spite of their lively friendliness, his eyes still seemed to be shuttered with glass.

"Life," he said, "is strange. That is a platitude, but I do not mind them. I use them all the time. I sometimes believe they represent the true international auxiliary language far more effectively than do Volapük, Esperanto, or Ro. I say that life is strange in this instance because of the conference that I have just gone through."

He accepted a glass from Murray and waited for Miriam to say, "In what way?"

"In the disability of two parallel lines to meet—a modest barb of doubt, perhaps, that Einstein might be wrong. I refer to Dr. Crownin-shield and Dr. Stone. They formed their associationship from the very fact that their thoughts, their life's works ran on parallel tracks. Their bonds are of the strongest and most scientific nature, and still they cannot agree. You, my dear, were contention's bone."

Murcheson paused for a sip, and for a repetition of Miriam's question, and then went on.

"Stone has been openly skeptical of several minor diagnoses of your affliction, diagnoses which have been offered as absolutes by Crownin-shield. I felt at times as though Stone were not questioning the master's dictums so much as that he was questioning the master himself. Almost as to whether Crowninshield were any longer to be considered a man capable of making analyses at all. There was the unspoken suggestion that Crowninshield was approaching senility, if not already passing into it."

Murcheson glanced across the saloon for a moment at Stone. He smiled thinly.

"I put it down," he said, "as the normal and impatient impudence of the intellectual young. I also put it down to the state Kate's death seems to have plunged him into. His reactions to it amaze me. It is like seeing a fine piece of mechanism such as a watch drop and break, with its intricate organisms flying apart in a hundred different directions. Fortunately it was I, by my layman's logic, who brought Stone finally into Crowninshield's camp." Murcheson drank at length. He wiped his mustache. "Odd, that. Wasn't it?"

"Yes. I wish you would tell me."

"I will. It was very simple, as such things sometimes are. I pointed out this. There is no evidence whatever that your life in California was under the faintest form of restraint. You were a free agent in the fullest sense of the term. *Nothing* but a mental affliction could have driven you to this bizarre and unnatural flight, because there was nothing from which you might have felt impelled to flee. Anything on earth that you had wanted to do you could have done normally, rationally, with prohibitory objections from no one. In other words, I reduced the argument to the absurd."

"You convinced Dr. Stone in that fashion?"

"Yes."

Miriam thought: That is not true. If Stone has shifted to a full agreement with Crowninshield, it is because he believes me to be Mrs. Vanesse's murderer and bases that on an aggravation of schizophrenia into one of the more homicidal manias.

Murcheson was going on: "Stone's agreement was somewhat grudgingly given, but it was there. Again I realized the upset condition of his emotions which at times threw him almost into a daze. And naturally I amplified. I have given you only my argument's core. The backbone of Stone's stubbornness was a belief that you had acted under a compulsion of fear, that you had fled California before some menace. I reduced that to its own absurdity, too."

"How?"

"Surely it must be obvious? Had fear at some peril driven you into flight from your home, your name, your secluded mode of living in which you were finding complete happiness and satisfaction, would you ever have voluntarily emerged from concealment? As you did emerge. Would you ever have placed yourself within the orbit of any family by the name of Murcheson? No. When I put it in that fashion Stone admitted that his doubts were unfounded, although he did so with remarkably poor grace. It was something like an animal who has been trapped in a corner from which there is no escape. After a little further pressure he drew up under Crowninshield's dictation a full history of your case to date. I am a stickler for documentary evidence. I have it in my safe. Will you join me in another highball?"

"Thank you, no."

"I believe I will—Murray! It was an arid session." Murcheson waited until Murray had refilled his glass.

He said, "I am afraid that we are in for a little bother in Baltimore. My intention was to lie at anchor only long enough to arrange that Kate have the services of her church and her body be cremated. Such was her wish. We shall carry her ashes with us to Palm Cay. That is all right. It is Stone who is the bother. He is not satisfied that Kate committed suicide. He is determined to insist upon an investigation of some sort which may delay us."

Murcheson's fingers tightened about his glass. He did not look at Miriam but held his eyes lowered upon the amber fluid of his drink. Ice cubes clicked.

He said, "You are not to worry. We shall do what is best for you, Jennifer. In spite of yourself."

CHAPTER 22

During the succeeding hour Miriam went below to her cabin and took stock. The case history of "Jennifer Murcheson," attested to by one of the country's leading psychiatrists and his assistant, was in the bag. In Murcheson's safe. The locket would also undoubtedly be in the safe. So the murderer's field work was done. Nothing remained but her (Miriam's) eradication from the scene.

How best to guard against the night?

How best in this sea-encircled coterie of a murderer and his blindly willing helpers to find shelter against the alert opportunism of a waiting death?

How best to live until the coming day would bring Baltimore and its contact with the world ashore?

The bolt on the cabin door, an inch or so of cylindrical brass, was her sole bastion for defense. Her fortress against the night's dark siege.

Miriam went over and turned the bolt's controlling knob. It did not stop at the point where the bolt would have been shot home. It went on turning. Around and around. A dark cloud curtained her eyes. Now it was certain. Now it was sure. She was slated for death before dawn.

Breaking the bolt had been a simple thing, as the arranged illness of the wireless man had been simple. She could demand that it be fixed, but would it be? Could it be? She could demand another cabin, but in face of the patiently detailed perfection of the murderer's whole course of work what would be the use? Some other cabin, some other device. Like that Swedish yeast which multiplies implacably from its own fecund self.

Ashore there were bureaus and tables and trunks, any number of things that could be employed for a barricade. In the cabin there were none. Beyond the futility of a couple of chairs, all other articles of furniture were either built-in or fastened down to conform with the exigencies of this world in constant motion.

The murderer's first weapon would be sleep.

Her eyes throughout the endless darkness of the coming hours must never shut.

In this moment, this nadir of despair with its lethargy of hopelessness, when even the smiles on faces and the willingness of helpful hands were weapons pointed against her, Miriam felt an overwhelming urge for having at least some future vindication. She rebelled at any exit from this life with the true story of her departure being forever unexplained. A desire for avengement was also present: if death were to come to her, her murderer must not escape.

She sat at a desk and wrote down everything that she had to say. When she had finished, the hour was half-past six. She sealed the pages in an envelope and decided to give it to Stone. Her obituary was penned.

Her thoughts were pellucidly clear (or so at least they seemed to Miriam), and she considered the problem of dress. In this hour when a danger loomed, one no less real because of its velvet invisibility, it was folly to ignore the slenderest safeguard that could be taken.

This extravagant and utterly foolish idea which rushed so heatedly about in her head brought the notion that the suitable dress for the night would be one that could be got out of easily, should a chance present itself to do so while struggling against the death grips of the sea. It did not appear foolish to Miriam, which of course it was. It did not occur to her that assuredly before she struck the water a blow would have rendered her incapable of any self-help.

Miriam selected a dinner dress of dark brocade, one which was easily unfastenable with a zipper. She arranged her face and her hair carefully, thinking that she might be doing so for the last time. The phrase was chilling misery. She slipped the letter under the bodice of the dress. She left the cabin and went up into the main saloon.

Murcheson was there alone.

He had dressed. He was standing with his back toward Miriam and facing the Empire case, while attempting in spite of the yacht's erratic motion to make it play. It occurred to Miriam as symbolic that the recording should again be the somber, nerve-shaking opening of Beethoven's "Fifth," with its paean of sable victories tragically won. Victory. Miriam thought: For Murcheson? His dark deed to all purposes already accomplished?

A lurch of the ship sent the needle screeching across the record, and Murcheson shut off the machine. He did not turn for a moment, but stood with his hands pressed upon the cover of the case. He sighed.

He said, in perfect awareness of Miriam's presence, "That was Kate's favorite. I bought the album especially for her, for this trip. Murray will bring cocktails shortly, Jennifer."

He came over and smiled at Miriam and offered cigarettes. She took one, and he lighted it.

"We are to miss the worst of the storm," he said. "Captain Liggett states that its path is veering toward the north. The night will be unpleasant, but we will get our rest. There will be no extreme turbulence to interfere with sleep." Murray came in with canapés. Murcheson arranged several on a plate and offered it to Miriam.

He said, "There are so few of the gray eggs left."

"Thank you."

"I have always been amused by Webster's social commentary on caviar. Do you know it?"

"No."

"'Caviar,' it states, 'considered a delicacy by some, is seldom used and little relished by the masses.' I consider the commentary entirely gratuitous, most un-American, and somewhat subversive. It should be brought to the attention of the Dies committee."

"And all Websters burned in a pyre?"

"Yes. I shudder at the repercussions among our national trade unions were they to unearth it."

Crowninshield, Stone, and Forsythe came in together. Cocktails were served while conversation revolved around the weather, anecdotally following the storms-I-have-met line. Forsythe confined himself to a tirade against luxury liners which, he maintained, ceased in a stiff blow to be luxurious at all and were far more subject to antics than the worst old hog-bellied freighter. Stone claimed that his own worst experience with weather had come while flying from New York to Chicago through a winter's gale, an experience which Forsythe was unable to top. He had (Forsythe explained to Stone) a fear against flying that amounted almost to a phobia.

Miriam did not contribute. She felt feverish and was irritated with the constant surveillance that Crowninshield was subjecting her to. He had, again, a twittery look. There was no opportunity for having a private moment with Stone. He absorbed himself matching gales with Forsythe, and whenever chance did face him toward Miriam he would shift his eyes rapidly and his mood would become implacably granite. She considered that his whole attitude would have made a fit model for Borglum to slash out from a mountainside, preferably on Storm King, brooding over the Hudson.

The death of Mrs. Vanesse, her body, the cabin which held it, were subjects carefully avoided.

They went in to dine. Storm fiddles racked the table's rim, and Branch did miracles with the serving. Crowninshield was seated on Miriam's right.

She said to him perversely, "How is Simmonds?"

"Simmonds?"

"The wireless operator."

"Ah, yes, poor chap." Crowninshield managed to capture some green-turtle soup. "I am puzzled. His symptoms could suggest several diagnoses, as symptoms do—more frequently so than it is good for the layman to realize." He smiled at Miriam warmly. "That is a trade secret. There is intestinal disturbance and probably inflammation. A toxic condition of some nature. I shall be glad to get him to Baltimore. This soup is delicious. A proper cenotaph for a turtle."

So the wireless set was still inoperative. Even had it not been, it was now too late. Course followed course. An entree of plover, a roast. A green salad, and a flaming dessert by Spinoff out of what once had been called St. Petersburg.

It was over coffee and liqueurs in the main saloon that Miriam managed to single out Stone. It was not easy to do, as he seemed to be consciously avoiding her. Crowninshield had bullied Forsythe into a bout of backgammon, and Murcheson had joined them at their table to watch the game.

Miriam sat in an armchair with its back toward the players. She took the letter from her bodice and held it in her lap.

She said to Stone, "Will you take this quickly, please, and keep it safely until tomorrow?"

Miriam had lowered her voice to a conspiratorial pitch, even though they were seated at the further end of the room from the backgammon table. Stone looked back at her in puzzled amazement. He reached for the envelope and held it in his hand.

She saw Stone's look shift to something behind her chair. "Some document that you value, Jennifer?"

A shock seized Miriam as Murcheson moved from in back of the chair and stood between them. His brown, glassy eyes studied her face for an instant and then settled on the envelope in Stone's hand.

Stone said, "Perhaps you had better place it in your safe, Mr. Murcheson? Miss Murcheson is worried about its security."

"I will be glad to."

Murcheson took the envelope from Stone.

Miriam felt weak from this sheer continuance of frustration. She said, knowing that whatever she said would not be of the slightest use, "It is not important enough for that."

"Everything of yours is of importance, Jennifer." Murcheson slipped the envelope into an inner pocket of his jacket. He placed a hand lightly on Miriam's shoulder. "I am sitting up with Kate tonight after I have had a little rest. Forsythe will also be with her for a while. I feel that it will take the edge off loneliness and help her on her journey." His eyes clouded. "Her long, long journey."

He left them and went out of the saloon.

CHAPTER 23

The rattle of dice at the backgammon table was staccato through the sounds of the wind and sea. Miriam heard Crowninshield offer a double and Forsythe accept it. She knew that Stone was observing her intently.

He said, after a while, "What was in that envelope, Miss Murcheson?"

"The truth."

"What new version of it, please?"

Miriam's eyes scalded with tears.

She said brokenly, "Don't be so damned superior. *Please* don't. Can't you see that you are all I've got?"

Miriam stood up. She went swiftly from the room. She knew that Stone was following her and that both Forsythe and Crowninshield had regarded her with sharp interest and speculation as she had hurried past. Tears were hot, almost blinding, and the motion of the ship would have sent her stumbling down the companionway if Stone had not caught and helped her. She had stopped crying by the time they reached her cabin. Stone went inside with her and turned on lights. He closed the door.

"I think, Miss Murcheson, we should have a little talk."

"What would be the use?"

"I don't want you to think of me as being what you said. Superior. I have just now seen your human side. Your face is wet with the first emotion that I know comes from your heart."

Stone walked over to the bed. He tried to turn himself into an automaton, some precision machine of steel. One among whose springs and cogs no space existed for a heart.

He said flatly, "Mrs. Vanesse died here. Tell me about it."

"Has Biddle spoken to you?"

"Biddle? Of course she would notice things, too. No, Biddle has said nothing to me. I came in here to investigate while you were up above with her this morning in the main saloon. Your arrangement of the bed and pillows was the customary work of the amateur. The position of the milk pitcher was improbably arranged. There were several things."

It was not herself who was speaking, nor he who was questioning her. Two other people were doing this. Two empty shells that were strangers.

This could be so. You could love a person and still stand away from it. Something could insulate you from that love and all of its warmth. But nothing could destroy it.

She said, "You are satisfied that I killed Mrs. Vanesse."

"No, I am satisfied with nothing concerning your aunt's death, Miss Murcheson, beyond feeling assured that she did not take her own life." He drew a chair up beside Miriam and sat down. He leaned forward. He looked at her intently. He repeated: "Tell me about it. Better me than the authorities in Baltimore. You will have no other course."

Miriam searched in Stone's expression for some glimmer of a human and sympathetic interest. His control was great enough so that she found none, saw nothing but a professionally probing regard held in readiness to lance and to dissect whatever statements she would have to offer.

She said, "Mrs. Vanesse rapped on the door. I thought it was another warning note. I unbolted the door and opened it. Mrs. Vanesse came in and fell back upon the bed. She said, 'Do not be afraid of me. Put your head down. Here.' One of her hands had been holding a fold of the dressing gown over the hilt of the knife. Mrs. Vanesse died, and this hand slipped down by her side. I saw the knife."

"What prevented you from calling for help?"

"I would have been accused of murdering her. You now believe that I did murder her."

"Disregard my beliefs, please. Why did you think as you did?"

"Dr. Crowninshield had warned me that a schizophrenic condition could be aggravated into an impulse to kill. To kill either myself or others. He is satisfied that I am Jennifer Murcheson and that I am insane. You are also now satisfied about it… Mrs. Vanesse was there dead, with a knife in her chest. Her body was alone with me in my cabin. How could I have reasoned otherwise, Doctor?"

"What was your next move?"

"I bolted the door. I sat down. I felt increasingly ill." Miriam flashed at Stone suddenly: "Can't you see that I was terrified? Driven almost into a stupor from plain terror?"

"We will get along better if you remain calm, Miss Murcheson. What is this warning note you referred to?"

"That came the night before last. There was a knock, and I found the note shoved under the door."

"Did you see who was outside?"

"I didn't open the door until later. I was interested in the note. The message was unsigned. It said that the writer believed in me and would try to help me. It warned me against taking any step that would prove irremediable. The word impressed me. It stated that I was in the most desperate danger. That murder was its root."

"Let me see it, please."

"I burned it. It said to. It said that if the note were discovered and the handwriting traced, the writer's life would pay the forfeit. I thought for a while, heedlessly, that it had been sent by you."

Stone's expression did not change "Was the writing in any way familiar?"

"No. I don't think it was disguised, but I do remember thinking it might have been written with the left hand by a right-handed person. It had that 'something wrong' about it."

"Close your eyes, please."

"Why?"

"Do as I tell you, Miss Murcheson. Thank you. Now try to evoke a mental image of that note. Did the letter formations seem to be angular or rounded?"

"Angular, rather."

"Think of some word you recall being in it that contains the letter *I*."

"Yes—"

"How is it divided? Is the upper part of the *I* longer than the lower part, or the other way? Or are they even?"

"The lower part is much longer. There is hardly any upper part at all."

"How are the *ts* crossed? With a firm stroke, or weakly?"

"Weakly."

"Thank you. Those are characteristics which would remain constant whether the wrong hand were used or not."

"Then you do believe I received that note?"

"Let us go on. Please repeat what you tell me your aunt said just before she died."

"'Do not be afraid of me. Put your head down. Here.' I realize that it doesn't make any sense."

"It makes excellent sense. What time did she rap?"

"I don't know. I should say about an hour after I had said good night to you."

"That would be at one. How long did you remain sitting in this 'stupor of terror,' Miss Murcheson?"

"I don't know that either. I heard five bells being struck after I had carried Mrs. Vanesse into her cabin."

"She was a large woman, a heavy one."

"I managed it. I closed her eyes. I covered the hilt of the knife with her dressing gown. Those were the two things which puzzled you. Surely my admission that I did them erases your doubts about suicide?"

Stone said with maddening patience, "My dear Miss Murcheson, your aunt was a most fastidious woman. Could any power of despair, however dark, have driven her to creep in secret to the galley for such a brutal, common medium as a kitchen knife to put an end to misery? Other measures were at hand, ones far more compatible with her nature."

"There was the sea, of course."

"There was the sea, as you say. My own thought is that her medicine cabinet is stocked with an opiate she had the habit of taking for her nerves. An overdose would have done the trick. Such would have been her selection had she proposed to take her own life. Not a kitchen knife." Stone paused for a moment. He weighed some speculation in his mind. He said, "Why did you close her eyes?"

"I liked her."

"Yes, she had stood up for you when you were young."

Miriam said with a fatalistic patience that equaled Stone's, "My only knowledge of Mrs. Vanesse has been the few moments we have spent together on board. My longest talk with her was yesterday afternoon on deck when she told me an anecdote concerning the theft of a locket."

Stone said with sharp interest, "Tell me everything you can remember of that talk."

"Mrs. Vanesse asked me to sit with her on the settee. She said that she was lonely."

"Lonely—try to recall her exact words, if you can."

"I think she expressed it as being 'the oddest attack of loneliness' and that loneliness could be classed as an illness, one which she had suffered infrequently. I suggested there were many remedies for it, and I remember her saying, I have known when there were none.'"

"You are certain of that? I find it most important, Miss Murcheson."

"Yes, I'm certain. Mrs. Vanesse went on to illustrate her point with the anecdote about a locket. When she was seven years old she formed one of those lifelong friendships with a girl called Edna. She discovered that Edna had stolen a large heart-shaped silver locket from a mutual friend, a girl called Beatrice, who was six. It would be an impertinence, I presume, to point out any associationship between that locket and that anecdote with the locket which so cleverly proves me to be Jennifer Murcheson? Which proves, so miraculously, the impossible?"

"Really, Miss Murcheson, the locket is but incidental to a chain of proof."

"All right. I'll go on. Mrs. Vanesse was in terror of telling Edna that she knew of the theft. She was afraid that Edna would be overcome with remorse and seek a watery grave, but eventually she did tell Edna. Edna gave her and Beatrice a sound slapping and kept the locket. Edna terrified them further with the threat of scratching out their eyes and feeding them to the cat if they told on her. Mrs. Vanesse said that then was when she first tasted loneliness."

"Her exact words as nearly as you can, please."

"She said that the loneliness was of the type for which there is no remedy, that her trust and love had been crushed under an insensate heel and that her world was emptied of everyone but herself. That she was alone. You will forgive me for referring again to the associative connection between the locket in her anecdote and the locket which was left in here on that bed table over there last night?"

"Do not harp on the obvious. Her words are of far greater significance than the locket associationship."

"I fail to see why."

"You are not a psychiatrist." The full implication of what Miriam had said suddenly struck Stone. "Did you just tell me that a locket was *left in here last night*?"

"How else would my fingerprint be inside of it?"

"I must beg of you to tell me the truth about this."

"The locket was on that table when I returned from carrying Mrs. Vanesse to her cabin. It had not been on the table when I left here. I opened it and looked at the miniature. I felt confused and ill. I dropped the locket back on the table. I washed a bloodstain from my nightgown, and the sight of the blood sickened me further. I fainted. I realized just before losing consciousness that I had failed to turn the bolt locking the door. It was morning before I came to. The locket had been taken away. You will not believe me, but that is the truth."

"My belief or disbelief is of no consequence, but the psychological significance of everything you tell me *is* of consequence. Return, if you will, to this talk on deck with Mrs. Vanesse. What was her manner?"

"I thought at the time that she seemed furtive. I remember her looking right and left as if she wanted to reassure herself that she would not be overheard. She did this just before talking about the locket, and again when she asked me about the mole."

"Mole?"

"She asked whether I had ever had one removed, a small one, scarcely noticeable, from here on the throat. When I assured her that I hadn't, her face changed frightfully for a moment. She looked at me almost with dread. It only lasted a second, this look, and then she said she was certain that her memory was false, that there had been no mole. Possibly you noticed Mrs. Vanesse's expression yesterday just before she fainted at lunch? It was like that."

"I am beginning to understand the cause of that faint. I am beginning to understand a good many things."

"Are you beginning to have some belief in *me*?"

"I must keep stressing that that is of no importance." Sudden tears again shook Miriam into incoherency.

"I suppose it's of no importance that the bolt on that door has been tampered with—that it has been purposely broken to simplify the murderer's job of coming in here tonight and killing me?"

Stone stood up. He made no effort to check her sobbing. He glanced at his watch.

He said, "Nothing now is of importance except time. It is ten o'clock. You contend that that bolt has been put out of order to simplify some attempt upon your life. I suggest that you remove those traces of tears from your face and go back to the others in the main saloon. Stay there. I will rejoin you after I have sent a message and received its reply."

"You understand wireless?"

"Yes."

"Tell me—at least you can do this—who are you sending to?"

She thought that his look softened a little. She realized it was from pity.

He said, "The police."

Stone left the cabin and closed its door.

CHAPTER 24

He had said, "to the police." He had said that it was ten o'clock, and that time alone was of importance now.

Miriam wondered whether Stone considered time of importance to him or to her. She evaluated what had been gained in her talk with him. Not very much. He thought her perhaps in peril, of sorts. But he had thought that right along, according to Murcheson, and had attributed her flight from California to some such menacing source.

The locket incident seemed in no sense to have convinced him that she was not Jennifer Murcheson. Why then was time of importance? She felt herself shivering.

It remained of importance to her. The slow pacing of every minute was drawing her closer to her fate. She phrased it just as melodramatically as that even to herself. There would be a meeting, and she held no doubt whatever but that it would be with death. She began to understand the psychology of men who when faced with the imminence of oblivion preferred to hasten the inevitable moment by taking their own lives. To get the torture of suspense over with.

One source of warmth alone remained in this chill of dread. Her love for Stone. Her answer at last seemed clear: to insist on staying with him until day. That would be it. When the others had retired, when (specifically) Murcheson and Forsythe would have retired and the yacht would be given over to its special sounds of storm through the long dark hours, during that inert timeless stretch between sleep and waking which murder found so suitable to its purpose, she would insist on staying with Stone.

A sense that was almost one of peace and security came over Miriam, and she removed tear traces from her cheeks and then hurried in a swift recurrence of panic from the cabin and back to the main saloon.

The backgammon game was over and Murcheson, Forsythe, and Crowninshield were drinking highballs. Miriam perceived an elaborate ignoring on their part of her recent flight from them in tears. She imagined that, the performance had been satisfactorily explained away by Crowninshield as a natural adjunct to her unstable condition.

This was perfectly correct. Crowninshield had brushed aside suggestions which had come from both Murcheson and Forsythe that he give Miriam some medical attention. Murcheson had been specific on the point and had insistently urged that she be compelled to take an opiate and so restore her obviously shattered nerves with a good night's sleep.

Crowninshield had refused. Such alarums and excursions were, he had said, to be expected and even had some therapeutic value as outlets from her pent-up state. He considered them in a sense as a healthy elimination of mental excrescences, comparable to the bodily function of sweating.

Miriam noted that Murcheson was at his most solicitous. He walked over to her and offered his arm as a prop against the pounding motion of the yacht and led her to a chair at the backgammon table. No one's eyes could have been kinder. Even the effect they gave of being lightly filmed with glass had lessened, and his voice held the warmest and most friendly of tones.

"Sit here, Jennifer," he said. "I am glad you came back. We need a fourth at bridge. You will forgive me for being the tyrant and insisting that you play. It will take the minds of all of us off many things."

He removed the backgammon board and replaced it with cards and score pads. He spread one of the decks.

He said, "It will be a long night. As I am sitting up with Kate I shall need an hour or two of rest. Shall we set a time limit on the game? Shall we say midnight?"

They selected cards, and Miriam drew the ace of spades. Chance, she thought, had rarely gone in for such a bromide. But it was in keeping, too: as run-of-the-mill as the pattern of the princess with her mole.

Only the setting was unfavorable to the scene. It was far too elegant and should have been replaced by a barren heath, a cauldron, and, of course, a witch. Would Crowninshield do? He alone was a proper age for witching. He had drawn the next highest card and had sat down facing her. Miriam glanced across at him and caught the bright pink smile on his lips and the amused air of tolerance with which he looked first at the ace of spades and then at her. "Curious," he said, "the persistence of a superstition."

It was a shock to hear Murcheson turn on him almost savagely and say, "That's luck. The ace is turned upside down. That means that all her ill fortune is leaving her."

"Does it matter what it signifies? My basic contention remains that a superstition is impossible to kill even in the face of the most outraged cries of common sense. The world would be decimated overnight if there were anything in them. I mean specifically if everyone who drew an ace of spades tonight were to die. Or if ill luck were to become literally active as a result of the other popular favorites. Surely, Mr. Murcheson, you must agree?"

"I will concede only that superstition does not exert its powers except among those who believe in it." He turned again to Miriam and said earnestly, "You will remember what I have said? That upside down the ace of spades means nothing but the greatest of good fortune? I know that you are one of the believers, Jennifer, because I saw you pale."

"I did?"

"And now," Forsythe said, "you blush. The perfect Victorian. I hasten to add in everything but looks."

"I thought Victorian women attractive."

"No, they had too much base."

Miriam dealt, and the game proceeded without incident.

An hour passed, and they noticed increasingly the effects of the storm, the tail-whip of which was beginning to lash the yacht. The wind had ceased its moaning sound and had developed an accent of shrillness.

An ash tray slid from the table and emptied itself on the floor. They stopped playing while Forsythe got up to ring for Murray.

"We are beginning to get it," Murcheson said. "I can reassure you, Jennifer, that the *Donna Louise* is sound. She has been through far worse weather than we are likely to catch tonight, and Liggett is an excellent man. He has salt water, not blood, in his veins."

Forsythe stumbled and just saved himself from falling as he returned to his chair.

He said, "This makes me consider the blessings of the poor. Only the rich have the chance to spend a fortune on a yacht, in order to suffer a beating such as we're in for. I envy the simple stolidity of the humblest shack."

"Providing," Murcheson said somewhat unpleasantly, "that you could observe it from a seat in the third row on an aisle."

"Perhaps you are right. Most of the truly enjoyable things in life are reproductions. Any sort of personal creation presupposes an amount of pain. And aren't I the one! I never realized, Jennifer, there were such depths in me. Did you? Why, I'm practically unplumbed."

"It sounds perfectly disgusting."

"Doesn't it? All loose."

Murray came in, and Murcheson said to him, "An ash tray overturned on the rug. Will you clear it up, please?"

"Certainly, sir."

"How are things below?"

"Not bad, sir."

"See that everything is made fast in the cabins, will you?"

"I have, sir. Everything is secure."

"Good."

Murray left, and the game was resumed. It was nearing midnight, at a moment when Murcheson was dealing, that Crowninshield speculated idly as to where Stone had been keeping himself.

"He intended sending a message," Miriam said. "He is probably still waiting in the wireless room for a reply." Instantly Miriam caught the tension that held Murcheson motionless, checking his hands in the middle of the deal.

"I was not aware that operating a radio transmitter was one of Stone's accomplishments," he said.

Crowninshield said, "He included it among his many extracurricular interests while on the medical examiners' corps."

"I do not like it."

"Really? Why not?"

"I have no doubt but that he is communicating with Baltimore. He is obsessed with his stupid notion that Kate did not take her own life. He will cause endless trouble and subject us to interminable delays. If I had known of this I would have asked Liggett to forbid him the use of the set. Now it is too late."

Forsythe said equably, "What difference does it make? He would have communicated with them anyhow as soon as we had dropped anchor."

Murcheson stood up.

"I had hoped to persuade him before then that he was mistaken. I shall say good night. I suggest, Jennifer my dear, that you also turn in. Tomorrow will be a dreary, a nervous day. If you will be so good as to consider the game closed and add up the scores, Dr. Crowninshield, I shall settle my share of it in the morning."

Murcheson walked toward the door.

He said, just before he left the saloon, "I regret this small display of impatience. There is no thought in my mind of impeding justice. Should justice be required. Come with me, Forsythe."

"Certainly."

Forsythe said good night to Crowninshield and Miriam. He said it was only natural that his uncle should be somewhat nervously unstrung.

He followed Murcheson out of the saloon.

CHAPTER 25

Miriam felt an interim of security while Crowninshield totaled up the scores.

It was, she considered, the essence of the murderer's plan that there be no witness to her killing, not even one who could be eliminated simultaneously. Certainly not Crowninshield, whose expert testimony as to her schizophrenic state would positively be required.

She wanted to prolong this moment of armistice until Stone would finish his business in the wireless room. Otherwise she would have to force herself upon him up above. She observed the neat exactitude with which Crowninshield finished the job.

He said, "I am inclined to agree."

"Agree with what, Doctor?"

"With your uncle. Stone is in the mood for trouble. I am fully aware, of course, of the origin of his present emotional upsets. When it hits a man of his special temperament it hits him hard and drives him into a state of outraged bewilderment."

"When what hits?"

"Oh, come, Miss Murcheson. Come, come. I still retain the services of my five senses. I, too, can kibitz. You love him, don't you?"

"Yes."

"Good. Very well, then. What are you going to do about it?"

"Nothing, that I know of."

"Nonsense. You are up against a tough proposition. Perhaps an impossible one. Again I ask you what are you going to do to resolve it?"

"What's tough about it? I understand there's a pattern for such things. I yearn and wait. Eventually he asks me to marry him or eventually he doesn't."

"Such a procedure with a man like Stone would get you nowhere. I return to the toughness of what you face. To begin with, he has no idea that he is in love with you."

"Is he?"

"He must be. Otherwise he is suffering from a severe case of nervous indigestion, and that is impossible because his appetite is excellent. You may recall that at dinner tonight he requested a second plover and went in heavily on the roast."

"Well, then."

"No, Miss Murcheson, it remains far from being well. There is the barrier between you of a doctor and his patient, a patient who remains to be cured. There is the question of married compatibility. Remember that he is acquainted with your case history, with that rather equivocal personality which we are striving to restore to you."

"According to Mr. Vanesse, Miss Murcheson was a hellcat."

"Precisely. Juxtapose it, as Stone must of necessity do so, with his career. When you recover this unbridled and willful other self, he must ask himself whether or not he can tame you. Can he take the time to do so? So that you will fit in as a suitable helpmeet with the calm and dispassionate scientific outlook he must maintain toward life?"

"This is perfectly fascinating, Doctor."

"You consider it with levity. I suggest that you do not. Lastly, there is the question of your rather staggering wealth. Stone's own family is far from being without means. His father owns silk mills which will, I presume, specialize in powder bags and parachutes for the duration. Eventually Stone will be endowed with a considerable fortune, but it will remain nothing in comparison with yours. A situation such as that is bound to irk. Stone is far from being the man to give up his pants."

"I should hope not. And aren't you an iconoclast, Doctor? I thought that love conquered all."

"The conquest, when it does occur, is generally a brief one. Little is so evanescent as the tint of rose in glasses. However, I am old and I am sentimental. While the tint remains, there is hope. I am also very tired. You will forgive me if I retire?"

"Of course, Doctor."

Crowninshield stood up.

"My advice to you is a bold, a frontal attack. Cut all wordage to a minimum. I have observed one thing about romance from my stand on the side lines, Miss Murcheson. It is this. You can talk yourself out of love."

Crowninshield smiled at her with kind sweetness and left the saloon.

He also left Miriam a good bit openmouthed. A phrase in favor during her mother's day recurred to her: her heart upon her sleeve. Was her feeling for Stone so obvious? That is, damn it, to everyone but Stone? And what good would it do? What good would anything do her five fathoms down, or whatever the depth of the surrounding ocean happened to be?

This gloomy thought revived her fears in the liveliest fashion, and the dangers inherent in solitude sprang out and appalled her. She decided to seek out Stone at once. The saloon, now empty, was inimical in spite of its charm and lights.

Miriam found it difficult to open the door onto the deck. She had to force it with all her strength and then almost recoiled before the sound and fury of the night. A slash of spume drenched her face, and the berserk stridency of the wind seemed the scream of idiots on the loose.

She reached the ladder to the bridge and clung desperately to its railing as she made her way above. Captain Liggett blocked her, looming swiftly before her and seizing her by an arm.

He roared above the howling wind, "What folly is this?"

Miriam roared back, somewhat less efficiently, "I want to see Dr. Stone."

"I do not care what you want. You will return below at once."

"I won't. I want to go to the wireless room."

"You will do as I tell you. You will get down below immediately."

Liggett took a more practical grip and all but lifted Miriam bodily down the ladder and along the deck to the main saloon door, which he opened, and then managed to deposit her across the raised sill.

His roar did not abate: "Do not dare set foot again on deck, Miss Murcheson. I forbid it. Look there!" He pointed dramatically across the rail toward the invisible seethe of the furiously tumbling waters. "One slight misstep and you would lose your footing and be gone. We could do nothing to save you. It is a miracle that you managed to reach the bridge."

He slammed the door.

CHAPTER 26

Miriam trembled violently from chill, and she realized that her clothes were drenched. A change would take but a few minutes, but she considered it would also require going below and being alone in her cabin for a space of time, which, however brief, might be the very moment for which the murderer was waiting with such bland patience.

It would not be necessary to be alone. She could ring for Biddle, and take up again the battle of blackmail with Biddle while changing her clothes.

Lurching and stumbling as the *Donna Louise* took heavy impacts from the shock of seas, Miriam made her way down the stairs and into the passageway.

The door to Mrs. Vanesse's cabin was swinging.

It opened wide as the onslaught of a sea would lift the bow, and then would swing almost shut as the yacht, with a shuddering groan, would drop into the trough. There was a grim unseemliness to the dead about it, and as she stopped to close the door Miriam looked inside.

Forsythe was kneeling at the bed. His hands clutched the sideboard for support. His face was lifted toward Miriam, a face distorted and ravaged by the shattering ugliness of a grief that had been for too long under an iron control. Tears were still streaked on his cheeks and his breath came in dry, brutal sobs.

He said, "Don't go. I could not help this. I feel better for it. It is over."

"I'm sorry. Terribly sorry."

"Thank you. Thank you for having come. I had planned to ask you to sit up with me with her for a while. You did come for that? You came to stay?"

"Yes."

Miriam could not say anything else in the face of such grief. The cabin had an unearthly gloom. A single reading lamp burned on the wall over the bed, swinging in gimbals. Its shade was of pleated ultramarine taffeta, and it washed a dim and ghostly luminance down on Mrs. Vanesse's mask of calm death, from which all blood had drained.

Forsythe's face cleared as though from a tremendous relief. He stood up.

"You're very good. Very kind." He gestured toward the settee under the portholes. "Sit down, shall we? That is if we can. I've not met weather like this before, never on a boat of this small tonnage."

As he closed the cabin door a qualm of caution urged Miriam to insist upon his leaving it open, fastened on its hook, but he was immediately beside her and arranging a cushion to prop her more securely on the settee.

The qualm did not last, and the atmosphere of the cabin was imbued with an extraordinary peace which relegated into a disregarded background the violence of the elements outside. Miriam thought it arose from the presence of this calm dead woman, her body bound to immobility beneath the coverlet of silk.

Miriam did, however, consider that more light would have been agreeable to augment the single lamp's ethereal glow with its pallid washing back and forth across that waxen face as the gimbals counteracted the motions of the ship.

"I have always used the term civilized as a yardstick for behavior," Forsythe was saying. "You did a thing in a civilized manner else you didn't do it at all. I have been stupid."

"Why stupid?"

"Because being civilized means—I am speaking of the chi-chi and pseudo-sophisticated sense of the word."

"I know."

"In that sense it means a deadening of all true emotion. You ignore realities or else skate across them with a detached sort of supercilious grace that is supposed to be the height of something or other. With yokels it is being smart aleck. With sophisticates it is polish. Actually they are the same thing." Forsythe smiled at Miriam frankly. "That cry did me good."

"Does anyone really know you?"

"I doubt it. How could they? I am never certain that I know myself."

Miriam was aware of a strange communion of sympathy springing up between them, a flow of mutual understanding which had its wellsprings in the emotional nature and physical background of the *mise-en-scène*: the tumult of the storm, the quiet dead, the grief-ridden son, and her own fevered fears over what the night's final hours would offer. The moment was ripe for confidences, as some rare moments are.

She said, "How intimately do you know Mr. Murcheson?"

"Uncle? Scarcely more than you do, really. Mother and I would run into him at long intervals when we were either sailing or returning from abroad, but you know what such meetings are. Dinner at the Plaza, a show, an hour of picking up threads which are so slender that it is silly to consider they even exist. We had little in common. You have brought us more closely together than anything else ever has."

"Why?"

"Why on earth not? We bent every effort in our search for you. How else could we have acted?"

"From the little Dr. Crowninshield has told me, none of you had much use for Miss Murcheson."

"In a way that is true. Must you keep referring to your self in the third person, Jennifer? No matter how difficult we thought you, we were your nearest relatives. Surely you don't believe we could have just sat quietly by with folded hands and let you vanish?"

"Was it Mr. Murcheson who first brought up the question of schizophrenia?"

"I don't remember. Such a thought springs up suddenly during any discussion on mental troubles. You accept it, and develop it. You forget who originated it."

How long (she wondered) dare I force this? Forsythe was giving her, she knew, only half of his attention, and his answers had been indifferently automatic. His thoughts were obviously on his mother, for his eyes stayed drawn toward the bed.

"Did Mr. Murcheson decide on getting Dr. Crowninshield?" Miriam asked.

"No, I suggested Crowninshield. I know that. Mother and I had to sail from Lisbon, you see. We were there for a while before we could get passage. Naturally we were thrown in constantly with refugees. The town was a parrot cage of madness, with people either stripped down to nothing or else blazing with jewels. A-diamond-for-a-cabbage sort of thing. Mother hated it."

"I imagine that she would have."

"I found it exciting. I picked up a drinking acquaintanceship with a Viennese psychiatrist in the bar of the Braganga on the Rua do Alecrim. We lowered its wine level considerably during several sessions. Naturally he talked shop. It fascinated me."

"He knew of Dr. Crowninshield?"

"Yes, and had the greatest respect for him. He thought him the best man in America. He impressed his name upon me through liter after liter of not-bad port. So I at once suggested Crowninshield to Uncle Donald as the best man." The look of abstract sorrow left Forsythe's handsome face. His features underwent a minute, a sharp contraction, and then were bland. He turned directly toward Miriam and said flatly, "Why do you ask me these things?"

The communion of sympathy and the flow of a mutual understanding were gone before the electrical tension in Forsythe's attitude. It was a tension which he was doing his best to conceal, with small success. Peace was also gone from the cabin, and in its place sprang out a sense of evil which pervaded the room's close confinement like a decadent and invisible vapor.

All of the points were focusing on Forsythe, and Miriam felt with finality that the murderer was beside her. In all probability that bar in Lisbon had been the place where the plot had seeded and taken growth in Forsythe's mind. Perhaps being at first just an idle interest in the trade chatter of the refugee from Vienna.

She did not believe that the psychiatrist had been impressed by Crowninshield at all. Otherwise Forsythe would never have suggested him to Murcheson. Certainly, that is, not impressed with Crowninshield's recent achievements or standing. Surely the suggestion would have been there that Crowninshield was on the threshold (or had crossed it) of his dotage, and the Viennese would have endowed him with senility, just as Stone had felt waveringly compelled to do so.

So strongly did this conviction and this prescience of evil play upon Miriam that every instinct warned her toward immediate escape. The shiver of terror that shook her suggested an avenue for flight.

"I am cold," she said. "My clothes are wet from having gone on deck. I had meant to change."

Miriam smiled apologetically and would have stood up, but Forsythe leaned toward her and placed a hand lightly on her wrist. There was no pressure; his palm simply rested there, cool and with no sense of weight, but some protective and unseen guardian warned Miriam that the slenderest false move or note would close Forsythe's fingers about her wrist in a circlet of steel.

He said again, "Why do you ask these things? What have you on your mind?"

Miriam tried to continue smiling. The muscles of her lips were hard and tight.

"Pneumonia, principally."

"I am serious."

"And I have been curious. I still am. Dr. Crowninshield has told me a good many things, but not all."

Forsythe's palm remained carefully gentle upon her wrist. "What else would you like to know, Jennifer?"

(Careful now—a retreat would be more dangerous than an advance.)

"I would like to know whether it was Mr. Murcheson who considered the other women investigated by the Durney people. Whether it was he who rejected them and ultimately selected me."

"I find your phrasing curious, Jennifer. We did not 'shop about' for someone suitable. We searched for one person only. We searched for you. Uncle left the selection, as you call it, to me. He supplied the money for the investigation, and I gave my time. His own was fully occupied in establishing his foundation for social research."

The pause lengthened into complete silence. Forsythe's bland eyes never wavered in their suspicious study of Miriam's tranquil (as she was trying to keep it) expression. She no longer dared look back at him again. Her eyes turned toward the bed. Had it moved a little? That calm dead face? A shock of ice drenched her at this seeming quickening of the dead. It had not. It had been the wash of light, perhaps a slight loosening of the bonds that held the body firm beneath the coverlet against the pitch and rolling of the ship.

He said softly, almost as though he were announcing the obviousness of the fact to himself, "You know, don't you."

"I must go—really—I'm shaking like a leaf—these clothes are chilling—"

"You know, *don't you!*"

If she could slide her wrist away from beneath his hand—if she could spring for the door—she tried the wrist gently. Forsythe made no attempt to retain it. His breathing grew uneven. A strange mottled look appeared on his skin. "Marry me."

"No—"

"Marry me, Miriam."

"No!"

He said with an almost petulant desperation, "You fool—oh, you fool—"

His hands shot out and closed about her throat.

She struggled against the crush of his body, twisting and beating at him fiercely, feeling the hot, slippery sweat on his cheek.

Her face was darkening from congested blood when his death grip weakened. His hands fell to his side. He gave a cry of mortal terror.

"Don't, Mother—*no, Mother*—"

The body of Mrs. Vanesse, its retaining bonds loosed by the violent tossing of the yacht, had turned sideways and was sliding from the bed.

Forsythe fell cowering onto the floor, mouthing his gasping sobs against the rug, sobs that broke into the scream of a soul damned to all the agonies of hell as the body struck him and then lurched to rest against his side.

CHAPTER 27

Miriam fled from the cabin, where Forsythe continued to grovel in insane terror. She sped along the passageway and up into the main saloon, where a tableau confronted her of Stone and Crowninshield. Crowninshield had a dazed, stricken look. He seemed shrunken into a chair while Stone stood before him holding several radiograms in his hand. Stone's face was expressive of the most sympathetic regret, and both were far too engrossed over their own contretemps to cast Miriam more than a passing and incurious glance.

Her voice, still shaken with horror, was not under control.

"He choked me—he was choking me to death when the body slid from the bed and struck him—he's down there now—"

Stone said sharply, "Forsythe?"

"Yes. He would have killed me if his mother—if her body—"

"Stay here with Dr. Crowninshield." Stone swiftly tipped Miriam's chin up and looked at her throat. "Hmmm—yes."

He released her chin, dropped the radiograms onto Crowninshield's knees, and sprinted from the saloon.

Crowninshield shrank further into the chair. His eyes were pathetic from a dazed bewilderment. He held his beautiful hands out toward Miriam in helpless appeal.

"Miss Lake, my apologies can only sound cheap after all that you have endured. Thank God that you are alive." Miriam was shocked straight out of her hysteria. The sound of her name being spoken had never seemed beautiful, but it did seem so now, like clear, cold water when you are parched. All sense of terror left her like a fever gone, and her nerves relaxed to a point that left her limp. She sat down.

"I gather that Dr. Stone has decided to believe me."

"These radiograms have convinced him. Miss Lake, a grave injustice has been done you. I again thank God that a desperate menace has been averted. One to your life. As for myself, my work, I am finished. I am an old, a broken man. A fool of the worst and most dangerous order, because I am an intellectual one."

Miriam permitted Crowninshield the small luxury of sailing for several minutes on these seas of self-castigation. Confidence was gone, and with it the edifice of a lifetime. Nothing was left but the temple's hollow shell. A footprint, perhaps, perhaps two, placed by him upon the track-less desert of psychiatry. They, unless later winds were to efface them, might remain. But nothing more.

A sigh, a pause, gave Miriam her opportunity and she took it.

"Could I see those radiograms, Doctor?"

"I shall read them to you. They are from the police department of New York City; from an Inspector Wallace Murgatroyd, to be specific. He is a friend of Stone's. I must warn you that their general tone will strike you as being flippant. Inspector Murgatroyd held no realization of the tragic gravity of your situation or the deadly importance of the investigations Stone asked him to make."

"I don't care how flip they are, Doctor."

Crowninshield selected one of the message blanks and examined it.

"This one covers inquiries made at the home of Mrs. Tomlinson Mayford. Stone informs me that Simmonds had a lucid period tonight and suggested that Stone piece together some scraps of paper in an envelope in the wireless room's desk drawer. Many of the scraps were shaped into cornucopias. When assembled they gave Stone your melodramatic but perfectly legitimate message and Mrs. Mayford's address."

Joy brought a brief relapse into incoherence.

"Ida—dear Ida—a friend of Mother's. She's in her dotage now—I mean—"

"She is not, my dear, alone."

"I meant it nicely, Doctor—*nicely* in it."

"Thank you." Crowninshield adjusted his pince-nez and read: "'Mrs. Mayford states Miriam Lake is a daughter of Eustace and Florence Lake, both deceased, both Mayford's dear friends. Lake attended Miss Davidge's school and learned her curtsies at Dodsworth's. Lake rated space in social register until dropped for becoming professional model, Powers agency. Mayford agrees Lake must be some looker, claims Lake was sweet child but for vicious habit of reciting Lincoln's Gettysburg Address in toto. Describes Lake as slender, chestnut hair, hazel eyes, and a follow-me-lads flair if she knew what to do with it. Mayford wanted to charter coast-guard cutter and personally effect rescue. Is wiring protests against gross inefficiency F.B.I. directly to J. Edgar Hoover and is phoning New York *Times*. Pleasant old buzzard. Scared the life out of me.' The message is signed 'Wally.'"

Tears filled Miriam's eyes, and for a moment she cried unreservedly, while Crowninshield pretended not to notice her and fumbled around examining the other messages.

"This one," he said, "concerns the positions which you told me about, Miss Lake. It states: 'Powers agency and *Bazaar* both confirm Lake statements on jobs and times of service. Powers people feel story will get big publicity break as it covers all angles suitable to hammock and marshmallow trade. Claim Lake highly photogenic, especially gams.'" Crowninshield looked up. "I believe that to be a typographical error for gums and I cannot catch the allusion."

"Gams, Doctor. Legs."

"I must add it to my list." He continued reading: "'They want Lake to contact them on landing. Photos in their files confirm Mayford description and Murcheson's sense. Would shanghai her any day myself. Send phone number. Best love, but not to you. Wally.'"

"Wally," Miriam said, "should see me now. Just a moistened rat."

"This third radiogram had a curious effect on Stone. I pass the effect on to you, Miss Lake, for what it may be worth. He, well, snorted and used a phrase I find it impossible to repeat. But I give you the snort. It concerns a Mr. Floyd Meddleby."

"Floyd? But it couldn't—Dr. Stone couldn't know anything about Floyd."

"He did not. That is, not until he received this wire, which is self-explanatory." Crowninshield read:

> *Bazaar* executive suggested literary critic of *Accessories*, Floyd Meddleby, as a possible source of more recent information. Lake showed with him occasionally at literary cocktail blackouts. *Bazaar* claimed Meddleby and Lake rumored altar bound. Meddleby says not so. Says Lake is just a good old steady girl. Meddleby very bitter and prefers statuesque blondes, the damn fool. Meddleby sends deepest sympathies to Murcheson (in re Lake) and hopes Lake either gets choked or does choke. She must have slapped him down. Be sure to tell Lake I am just a good old steady cop, even if I do look like Adonis. Wally.'"

Miriam smiled warmly, and Crowninshield read the last of the radiograms.

> "'Only information obtainable from Bascombe Reed, Murcheson counsel, is that Murcheson finances are in A1 condition. Sister's fortune dissipated by her husband, deceased, Artemus Vanesse. Destruction by fire of house where Lake lived (and God knows why) arson. Suspicious character resembling male toothpaste ad noted by neighbor Marthe Fiorelli at five that afternoon. Have I asked you to give my warmest regards to Miss Lake? If not, I do. Wally.'"

Crowninshield folded and placed the radiograms in a pocket.

"Possibly in the goodness of your heart," he said, "you will find the sympathy, the kindness to forgive me. I can only say in self-defense that I found the evidence presented to me to be overwhelming. At least you will believe that what I did do I thought was for the best. For your best."

"I do, Doctor. Anyone would have acted as you did. Anyone."

Crowninshield cleared his throat sharply.

"Thank you, Miss Lake."

The door opened abruptly, and Stone came back into the saloon. His face was pale, and small muscles twitched in his cheek. He came over and stood before Miriam, almost consciously squaring off to face her.

He said, "I have no time now to tell you what a blow it was to me when I learned that everything you have said was the truth. In a way I am glad. Forsythe has escaped. That is, he is not in Mrs. Vanesse's cabin or in his own. It is possible that remorse has overcome him and that he has jumped into the sea. The yacht is being searched."

Stone took a small automatic from his pocket and handed it to Crowninshield. He said, "If you have to use this, use it promptly. Don't quibble. It is possible that Forsythe has armed himself, and you know that the actions of a man in his state of despair and terror are unpredictable."

Stone hurried out on deck, letting in great gusts of the howling wind.

Crowninshield examined the automatic with distaste and bewilderment. He said faintly, "I find that these confusions—that such rumpuses—"

Miriam reached over and took the gun from his hand. "Perhaps, Doctor, you had better let me handle this. Will you have some brandy?"

"Yes, my dear, I will."

CHAPTER 28

Crowninshield did not faint. He sipped brandy and listened attentively while Miriam gave him an account of her escape from Forsythe's lethal fingers. The final details which involved the movements of Mrs. Vanesse's body excited him tremendously from (he said) a psychological point of view. He considered that this culmination of her experience had an atavistic touch which reached back in an extraordinary fashion into the Dark Ages. He showed every intention of expounding upon this at great length, but Murcheson came in with Stone and interrupted him.

Murcheson went directly over to Miriam.

"I am completely stunned by this, Miss Lake, and shocked. It is a grim experience to find yourself in the role of a kidnaper, because that is exactly what all this amounts to. Apologies under such circumstances are childishly fruitless. I shall not insult your character, as I have come to know it, by offering any amends. I shall not contest any charges you care to bring against me when we reach Baltimore. I have injured you grossly and am willing, in fact I want to be punished for it."

"There will be no charges, Mr. Murcheson."

"I felt you would say that. Will you accept me as your friend? Will you permit me to help you, not only now but all through your life? You will take a great weight from my conscience if you will do this. I am not speaking only of money. You know that. That would be simple. There are many other things that a man in my position can do. I should like to guard and, well, to shelter you, Miss Lake."

"Thank you."

"The law will take care of Forsythe, unless he has already had the courage to take matters into his own hands. I doubt it. Dr. Stone doubts it. The first officer is continuing the search for him. Let me take that gun. I am positive you will have no use for it. Forsythe has always been a weakling and is probably cowering in some hide-out in a palsy of terror."

Miriam gave Murcheson the gun.

Murcheson continued to be distastefully bemused by Forsythe's weakliness and went on to say: "Artemus, his father, was also a weakling, although a brilliant one. A dilettante in the art of living charmingly. I could understand perfectly why Kate loved him and was willing to sit by adoringly while he scattered her money right and left. I had no idea how ably Artemus had done this until Kate confided in me after we had sailed how close she was to being penniless. It explains Forsythe's whole ghastly course of action. That is, it explains it to Dr. Stone's satisfaction if not entirely so to me. Why didn't Kate speak? Why didn't Forsythe come to me openly and say that they were broke?"

Stone said, "That would have been contrary to his nature, Mr. Murcheson. He knew you. You would have arranged a position for him. He would have had to work for his living."

"That is true. I would have."

"Your nephew has the impatience of all spoiled children, especially those of the rich. It did not satisfy him simply to kill his cousin and conceal her body."

Miriam asked, "Why not? Do you feel as I do that he was afraid a post-mortem would have proven murder?"

"Yes, I am certain you are quite right in that. But that was not all. You must remember that a lengthy and most careful search was made, and yet the body has never been found. I think he has disposed of it so successfully that it never will be found unless we can force him to tell us where it is. No, I think what activated him most was impatience."

"I don't understand that."

"Unless a body or proof of corpus delicti were offered, Forsythe would have had to wait for the prescribed number of years until the law would acknowledge his cousin to be legally dead. He was much too impatient for anything like that. He wanted to get his hands on her fortune right away."

"Was he her heir?"

"Not directly. His mother would have inherited, which meant to all purposes that he would have. Mrs. Vanesse never denied him anything. He wanted immediate results, which is why he schemed to arrange a substitute corpse which would be acceptable to the law. You were to have been that corpse, much as you deduced in your statement in that envelope. Mr. Murcheson and I have read it."

Murcheson said, "This is a damnable situation all around. If Forsythe has had the courage to jump overboard, I feel that we can never be certain that we know the truth. Whether he *has* killed Jennifer, or not. Whether he killed Kate. I cannot, I will not believe that he killed Kate."

"I can't think that either," Miriam said. "I saw him crying. That was real."

"Still," Stone said, "there would seem no other solution. We know he was responsible for leaving the locket in Miss Lake's cabin and for taking it away again. It is only reasonable that in order to do this he must have been aware of Miss Lake's movements. He must have known that his mother had gone into Miss Lake's cabin and he must have watched Miss Lake carry Mrs. Vanesse back to her own cabin. Finally, of course, he must have known that his mother was mortally wounded. And still he did not call for Dr. Crowninshield or for me to help her. Why not, unless it was he who had stabbed her?"

"Are you certain about the locket?" Miriam asked. "Can it be proved?"

"The prosecuting attorney will find no trouble with that. It is well attested to. When we were looking through Mrs. Vanesse's things for a suicide note we found the plain envelope holding the locket. As Forsythe had intended us to find it. The point is that that envelope never was put into Forsythe's hands. He was sitting in a chair at the time, presumably bowed down with grief."

"I still think his grief was real."

"I prefer to consider his performance as remorse. Dr. Crowninshield found the envelope and gave it to Mr. Murcheson to open. Mr. Murcheson promptly did open it and read the note. The significance of the enclosed locket was apparent. The thing is that at no time was that envelope or that note in Forsythe's hands."

"Why is that important?"

"Because we were to presume that not only had he never touched them but that he did not even know of their existence or of the existence of the locket. Still, this is what we found. Mrs. Vanesse's fingerprints were on the note, so we know that it was genuine. Fingerprints of Mr. Murcheson and of mine were also on the note. There were no fingerprints of Mrs. Vanesse on the envelope."

"Forsythe had taken the note out? He had put it back in a different envelope after getting my fingerprints on the locket?"

"Yes, and to clinch it, Forsythe's fingerprints were on both the note and the envelope."

"That seems stupid. I mean it seems contradictory to his careful elaboration of detail. I should think he would have worn gloves."

"You have missed the characteristic thread that ran through his scheme. The whole structure was built toward the ultimate success of your substitution for Jennifer Murcheson being accepted."

"Which it was."

"Yes. And then you were to be lost overboard at sea. The moment that that was accomplished, nothing previous to it would have been questioned, and certainly nothing concerning Forsythe. His Virginia alibi covering the day of Miss Murcheson's disappearance in California is in line with what I mean."

"Can you disprove it?"

"I think it will easily be disproved from the very reason that Forsythe was confident it never would be questioned. He is not clever. Not really clever. He gave himself away completely over that flight business."

"What flight?"

"Possibly you were not paying much attention to him tonight while we were talking about different storms we had gone through. This was just before dinner. He told me distinctly that he had a *fear of flying which amounted to a phobia.*"

"Well, I should think—"

"Think back, Miss Lake. Think back to yesterday, when Mrs. Vanesse fainted at luncheon. Naturally she would be aware of her son's dread of flying. It was her sole guard, her one haven of safety, this conviction that nothing could ever induce Forsythe to get into a plane. It made her feel he *must* have gone to Virginia, because to have gone to California and back, to have accomplished that formless horror in her fears, he would have had to fly."

"Duck—muscovy duck—"

"You're getting it. Even though Mrs. Vanesse was talking to Dr. Crowninshield, she was intensely concerned with everything Forsythe was saying to you. You were discussing muscovy duck, and he said this: 'The last time I had these ducks was *on a plane.* There was something rather poignant about it. To be in flight and eat the bird—' He did not complete the sentence. He noticed the effect his words were having upon his mother. She cried out and fainted, because she realized that nothing but business of the most desperate nature could have induced Forsythe to fly, and her fears throughout the past year were at last confirmed."

Richardson, the first officer, came in.

He said to Murcheson, "We have covered the ship. There is a possible chance that Mr. Vanesse could have slipped past us and be hiding in some spot we have already searched. We are going through her again."

"Thank you, Mr. Richardson."

"The decks are well patrolled, but I have been worried about you people in here. A man in his situation might be desperate."

"I think not. I know my nephew, Mr. Richardson."

"Well, just as you say, sir"

Richardson left.

CHAPTER 29

Miriam was not satisfied. There had been too many things in Mrs. Vanesse's actions which struck her as being out of character, things which a woman such as Mrs. Vanesse had been would never have done.

"There is one thing that bothers me," she said to Stone. "I suppose it is a woman's bother. You speak of Mrs. Vanesse's fears during the past year being confirmed. Would she keep silent, would she shelter even her own son if she felt him to be a murderer? Would she have stood by and let him go ahead if she thought the success of his plan demanded my death? She was a very human woman, a very fine one. I can't believe she would have done that."

"You must remember," Stone said, "that her fears were formless until the moment when Forsythe crystallized them by his statement concerning having taken a plane."

"But why have fears at all? Why have thought him a murderer in the first place?"

"I cannot answer you. No man can answer. I doubt whether anyone will ever solve the mysteries of a mother's instinct, her intuitive apperceptions concerning her children. This is especially strong with an only son. She 'knows' when he has been hurt. She 'knows' when he is troubled. She 'knows' it should he be in danger. No, Miss Lake, I can only be positive that fears did exist. Otherwise Mrs. Vanesse would not have written you that warning note."

"The details of the handwriting which I remembered were hers?"

"Yes. Look at it in this fashion. Mrs. Vanesse was quite literally on the rack and being torn in heaven knows how many directions. She was in desperate fear that her son was a murderer and that, if he were, his crime would be discovered, with the result that this child whom she worshiped would himself suffer the most ghastly of all deaths at the hands of the law. She was desperately eager to believe that his unforgivable crime (still problematical) had been committed for her sake and must thus find partial forgiveness or at least understanding in her own conscience. Does that make sense to you?"

"It is rather far-fetched, but I think it does."

"Furthermore, she knew that unless her fears were groundless, you could *not* be Jennifer Murcheson. So she was plunged into further terror that you were in danger of your life. That was a risk she refused to dally with at any cost. She would at least put you on your guard with that warning note."

"I still do not understand the part in which she said that if her handwriting were identified she would pay the forfeit with her life. She simply couldn't have believed that her own son would kill her."

"Could she feel certain? I think not. Could she have felt certain about anything? My own interpretation is that in the confused terrors of her mind lay the knowledge that if Forsythe were to identify the handwriting and then 'have it out with her,' she would have to denounce him publicly, and if the state were to execute him, her own life would no longer be worth living, so she would pay the forfeit by taking it herself."

Miriam was puzzled by this: "After Forsythe made that slip about the plane, which you say convinced Mrs. Vanesse of her fears, why didn't she warn me at once?"

"Consider the talk she did have with you at the first opportunity on deck. I feel it to have been a final despairing effort on Mrs. Vanesse's part to prove to herself that you *might* be Jennifer Murcheson in spite of all she intuitively believed to the contrary. Mr. Murcheson does not remember one way or the other, but I think that Mrs. Vanesse did know that Jennifer Murcheson had a small mole on her throat. As for the locket anecdote, she knew that that locket must have been one of Miss Murcheson's dearest possessions, in that it held a portrait of her father. Mrs. Vanesse devised the form of the anecdote to trap some reaction from you without exposing her own wretched beliefs."

"Surely when there was none it must have dissipated her doubt, her hope?"

"She had one life line still to cling to: the possibility that if you were Jennifer Murcheson, your lack of reaction to the mole and to the locket could have been due to schizophrenia. She was fighting up to the very end. I believe she felt there would be no danger to your personal safety until night fell, and she was determined before then to confront her son."

"You say determined?"

"Her actions suggest so. She retired early last night, at ten, although she was accustomed to staying up until after midnight. Forsythe played backgammon with Mr. Murcheson until eleven, when they said good night and went below. I think that Mrs. Vanesse during that hour permitted Leclos to attend to her customary duties of getting things set for the night, and that Mrs. Vanesse then went into Forsythe's cabin and waited for him to come below."

"But it was two hours later; it was around one o'clock before she came into my cabin."

"Forsythe spent part of that time talking in Mr. Murcheson's cabin until Mr. Murcheson went to bed. He then, I believe, stayed out on deck observing you and me through a porthole, waiting for you to go below. I think he then waited until after Murray had cleared up in here and had finished putting things away in the galley. By then it would be close to one o'clock. Forsythe then went into the galley and took the knife."

"He meant to use that knife to kill me."

"Yes. He knew, as everyone knew, of Dr. Crowninshield's fears regarding you. That a possibility existed of your killing yourself or of developing a homicidal mania. He intended to stab you and to arrange the scene to resemble a suicide."

"He did not know his mother would be waiting in his cabin."

"No, and I think that when he finally did reach his cabin and found his mother there he came in holding the knife in his hand. God knows what she must have thought or done, but I believe he struck her then."

The sudden sound of Forsythe's voice paralyzed them with shock.

"That isn't so. I did not kill her. I did not."

He looked already dead. His face was utterly devoid of color, and his body trembled from the devastating misery of a spiritual ague for which there was no relief. He had no weapon, either for self-destruction or for attack. He let the deck door close and came over to them. He sank weakly into a chair.

He said, "When Mother saw the knife in my hand she said nothing. I said nothing. Then with no warning whatsoever she flung herself upon me with a cry of despair and horror. We struggled, and she attempted to twist the knife from my hand, and a violent roll of the yacht sent both of us crashing to the floor. I lifted her up. The knife was sunk in her breast." His voice became a grating whisper. "I didn't kill her."

Stone said, "You might have saved her."

"No, I could not. You must think how I felt. Of what my mind was going through. Of how I suffered."

Every intonation was demanding that Stone sympathize with what Forsythe so evidently considered to be a predicament that had cruelly been arranged by fate to disrupt the smooth flow of his utterly useless and blindly self-centered life.

"I believed," Forsythe went on petulantly, "that to all purposes she was already dead, that nothing could have helped her. Agony, horror, both vanished from her face, which grew quite calm and smooth. She even smiled. The way the dead do. I must insist upon your believing me when I tell you that she smiled. It unnerved me completely. I went to pieces. I cannot remember ever before having been so badly upset. You cannot begin to imagine what I went through."

"I can better imagine what your mother was suffering."

Forsythe shook his head irritably and then said with the exasperated patience of an adult explaining the simplest thing to a child, "She suffered nothing. I have told you that she had lost all sense of feeling." Small beads of sweat had sprung up on his forehead and were moistening his livid cheeks. He said again, almost as though he wanted to convince himself of the fact rather than to persuade Stone, "I did not kill her."

"Then why did you have the knife?"

Forsythe looked weakly cunning. His eyes flickered toward Miriam.

"I had just taken it from Jennifer's hand. I met her in the passageway as she was about to go into her cabin. I could see that she was suffering a mental attack. I was afraid she intended to kill herself—"

"Stop it!" Murcheson cried sharply. "Stop lying! It was you who intended to kill her. Your clutching at schizophrenia and mental attacks is futile. Miss Lake is a thoroughly normal and sane young woman and her identity *as* Miss Lake has been proven."

This stunned Forsythe completely. His lower lip started to tremble.

"You can't have," he whispered. "There was no way—"

"Stone found a way. He radioed the New York police and has received replies proving that Miss Lake is everything she has claimed." Murcheson's voice grew harsh. "*Why* did you have to kill Jennifer? Why didn't you come to me? If you wanted money so desperately I would have given it to you."

Even though still stunned by the blow of Miriam's identity having been established, Forsythe managed a faint smile.

"Would you?"

"Of course. I would have taken care of Kate gladly. I would have found a position for you and put you on your feet. I would have made a man of you."

"Yes. I was afraid of that."

"I suppose you have arranged it to your own satisfaction that Jennifer's death was also 'accidental'?"

"I was in Virginia. You know I was in Virginia. I—"

"Stop lying, I tell you! Stone has punctured your alibi with phobias against flying and muscovy ducks, and—"

Anger made Murcheson incoherent, but Forsythe caught the significance of his uncle's statement. He started to go completely to pieces. He seized with swift desperation what he must have considered his final chance for escape: a maudlin attempt to convince his uncle of his,

Forsythe's, blamelessness and a subsequent hope that Murcheson would connive to shelter and help him in a flight from the law.

"I did not kill Jennifer. That was an accident too."

"You admit your presence on the scene. You admit that you know her to be dead."

"Because I want you to understand it. I want you to understand *me!*" Forsythe's words were broken shockingly by dry sobs. "You will believe me and you will help me? You will help me to escape? Yes, I was there. I did fly West. I waited on the trail where Jennifer had always taken her morning rides when she was a kid. It edged a crevasse."

He studied his uncle's face searchingly, striving to find some break of sympathy in its sternness. He went on feverishly, "I gave Jennifer her chance. I asked her to marry me. She struck me with her riding crop. She kept on beating me with it while I tried to defend myself and at the same time prevent her from falling into the crevasse, but she broke away from me and fell. I beat the horse and forced it in after. What else was there for me to do?"

Stone interrupted Forsythe's all but maudlin raving. "Mr. Vanesse— tell me, please, something about that crevasse. I find an unpleasant contradiction in the fact of it edging a trail along which Miss Murcheson was known to follow. I fail to understand why the body of the horse did not betray itself. You will understand what I mean." Forsythe wiped a film of sweat from his face.

"No, there would have been nothing like that. The crevasse is a freak formation. Local legend attributes it to some early earthquake. It is narrow, and no one has ever been known to plumb its depths. No one knows how deep the split is. The legend also has it that the crevasse is based by a stream which vanishes underground. I could hear nothing after Jennifer had fallen, after the horse had fallen—nothing—no sound—I stood there listening, rigid with horror at the accident—"

Murcheson said with disgust, "Your story is a subject for pity rather than the ridicule to which a prosecuting attorney will subject it. I suggest you do not advance it at your trial. The most moronic of juries would never believe you."

"No—no, they would not. But you must. You must help me!"

"You did not go there openly. You arranged an alibi and then went to the ranch in secret. You had but one purpose, and that was murder. Every step that has been taken in this warped, this foul scheme, can be traced to you."

Murcheson stood up in his anger and towered over Forsythe.

He said, "As Stone has pointed out to me, the very letter which you forged to establish Miss Lake's handwriting as being that of Jennifer's will damn you. I refer to the letter you claimed was received by you six years ago from Jennifer after her father's funeral, just as you and Kate were sailing to return to France. The establishment of Miss Lake's identity has given that letter the lie, just as it has given the fingerprint in the locket the lie."

A look of tragic sorrow swept Murcheson's face.

"Stone pointed those things out to me, Forsythe," he said, "just after we had put your mother's body back onto the bed."

It was Crowninshield (his recent confusions gone, now that in Forsythe a new specimen was excitingly presented for psychological dissection before his pince-nez) who cried: "Mortmain!"

Forsythe shook with terror. He looked at Crowninshield dully.

"What was that?" he asked. "The hand of the dead?"

"Mortmain, dear fellow. Again I am confounded by a phenomenon that lies beyond the boundaries of scientific reason. Surely you must recall that ancient practice in English law, that test for murder, where the accused was forced to place his hand upon the dead body of the victim? The body was presumed to inspire some 'sign' of innocence or guilt? Look at yourself in a mirror, young man. *The body of your mother struck you.* Go find a mirror and look upon the face of guilt, I tell you." Crowninshield's voice rose to a pitch of triumph. "You are lost!"

CHAPTER 30

Miriam hoped someday to be able to forget the spectacle Forsythe offered when he had broken down. He had lost all human semblance and had turned into a whining, groveling beast, alternately whimpering and snarling as Richardson had led him below to be kept under guard until he could be turned over to the police in Baltimore.

Miriam spoke of this with Stone while they stood on deck the following morning as the *Donna Louise* headed up Chesapeake Bay.

"You'd have done some snarling too," Stone said, "if you'd been in his state of mind."

"I hope never to be in that state of mind. It was disgusting."

"That's Annapolis over there. We'll land in a couple of hours. You may never be in that state of mind, but there's something wrong with you just the same."

"Oh, now look here, let's not start that all over again."

"This has nothing to do with schizophrenia. It is simply that you need readjustment."

"Why?"

"Haven't you felt so yourself? Haven't you ever asked yourself frankly what was wrong with you?"

"Really, Doctor. Is there anything?"

He said impatiently, "There is plenty. You're attractive, you are intelligent, and still you couldn't keep a job and you had no friends. Why?"

Miriam realized that Stone was serious and that what he said was perfectly true.

"I don't know why. As for the jobs, I suppose I just didn't have the ability. But as for friends—well, apart from Floyd—"

"You can skip that Meddleby quince. He doesn't count. I mean real friends and I mean everyday ones, not the little group you grew up with."

"Oh, they're all scattered, of course."

"Well, that's not unique. Who does keep in touch with the friends of his childhood nowadays? Very few do. Business takes them away, family requirements intercede. No, I mean the people you meet casually and come to like, if only for a while."

"Again I don't know."

"I'll tell you. You're something of an introvert, and that is further aggravated by your being a subconscious snob."

"I am nothing of the kind."

He told her not to argue about it, and then he went right on and handed her a good sound lecture. Never (he ordered Miriam) let the world pass by. Keep up with it. The Murray Hill part of her life was dead, so bury it, and stop clinging to any false fastidiousness, any minutiae of bygone standards. Stop also living in her memories. That sort of introspection was as fast growing a habit as an addiction for cocaine. And it could be almost as deadly. It would degenerate into a coddling sort of self-pity.

Whether she disliked the attributes of current-day living or didn't like them, at least accept them. He, for example, thought jitterbug music pathetic and just a little senile, especially when it would be gushed over by adults who were old enough to have quit playing with their toys.

But he had balance enough to know that the stuff was here to stay until it had run its course. As the bunny hug and other capers had run their courses. It was all right for kids, he guessed. Like this habit of taking off their shoes on a dance floor. He'd done things himself when young. He did not specify.

The lecture drifted over into their personal likes and dislikes. He had the same objection to chamber music as he had to jazz. He considered that four zealots sawing away at Bach was simply being precious about it and just annoyingly tiresome.

By the end of an hour they were warm old friends.

But they were also nothing else. Miriam thought about this while answering intelligently whenever Stone gave her a chance to. And she thought how right Crowninshield had been in his dictum that you could talk yourself out of love.

The bold, the frontal attack. That (still according to Crowninshield) was the proper stuff to give the troops.

Stone was saying: "Now painting is somewhat different. You can escape if the example of some genre offends you simply by closing your eyes or else turning away."

Miriam felt like saying firmly and clearly, "I love you," but she could not. So she concentrated on thinking it, in the tepid hope that there might be something in thought transference after all.

"But you can't," Stone said, "turn away from music. Circumstances usually arrange that you are trapped in a seat at a concert or something."

"I" (Miriam thought) "love you."

"Is there something the matter with you?"

"No. Why?"

"Then what are you screwing your face up for?"

She said stiffly, "Never mind." She said, that as that bunch of stuff over there was obviously Baltimore, she would go below and get ready for landing or whatever plans the authorities might have in view. She left him with the statement that she thought all music was stifling and that she was sick of it.

Miriam found Biddle in her cabin.

"I didn't know whether you'd care to have me help you pack or not, Miss Lake. Under the circumstances. I imagined you'd want to go right ashore. I took a chance."

"I have nothing to pack, Biddle."

"That's right. I didn't think of that. Can I say that I'm sorry, or wouldn't it mean anything to you? I feel like a skunk. I feel perfectly wretched."

"Don't. Don't feel anything about it."

"That's very good of you, Miss Lake. We're stopping. That will be the police launch coming alongside, I guess. I—I just can't help *crying*."

"Good. I'll join you."

The *Donna Louise* lost way and then shuddered as the engines went into reverse. Miriam let Biddle help her as she changed into the suit she had worn when she had come on board. The hat had stopped being limp and was quite good again. Then she said good-by to Biddle and went up above.

The main saloon was crowded with a group of people who were later identified to Miriam as United States Commissioner Bullman, his secretary, Mr. Johnson, several lads from the Baltimore police, a news-reel cameraman, and the press. Murcheson, Stone, Crowninshield, and Captain Liggett were all involved in separate official discussions, and Miriam realized with a pleasurable shock of surprise that Ida Mayford (magnificent in black broadcloth, a turret hat, and plenty of jet) was leaving a group of press photographers and bearing down upon her.

"My dear Miriam," Ida said, embracing her, "you have given me a new lease on life. I haven't been so stirred in decades. Come with me. Mr. and Mrs. Stone are naturally most anxious to meet you."

Miriam said stupidly, "His father and mother?"

"Yes. They're behind those pleasantly fresh reporters. Under that egg thing on the wall. I like the Stones very much. They haven't a particle of use for the Administration."

Mrs. Stone, in looks, was not unlike Ida. A little more motherly, perhaps, and with amber beads instead of jet. Mr. Stone was a gray-haired image of his son. Both of them appraised Miriam for a moment with a good long look, then Mrs. Stone broke into a pleased smile and kissed her warmly. Mr. Stone restrained himself to a good handshake and the thoroughly unrelated remark (so far as Miriam was concerned) that he knew that if his son lived long enough he would show some sense.

"The wedding," Ida said definitely, "will of course be held in my house, as soon as that hideous murder business has had time to settle. It will be the first event I've had there in fifteen years, since the fire department put that blaze out in Pewter's room. She smoked."

"What," Miriam asked, "wedding?"

Mrs. Stone looked stricken.

"Why yours, dear. Yours and Will's. Didn't Will tell you? He radioed us last night to be on hand to greet you. I'm sure he said to 'greet the imminent bride.'"

Mr. Stone said, "He did."

"Oh, I do—I *do* hope there isn't any mistake."

"Of course there isn't," Ida said. "I understand perfectly. It's the scientific mind. Haverstraw had it. He was that friend of your father's, Miriam, who first suggested plastics and went mad."

Mrs. Stone said with compassion, "My poor child—the life you're going to lead."

A voice rang authoritatively through the saloon. It belonged to United States Commissioner Bullman and effected an immediate silence.

"All right, now," Bullman said. "I'm ready to take your statements. Miss Lake, I'll begin with you."

ABOUT RUFUS KING

Rufus King (1893–1966) was an American author of Whodunit crime novels. He created four series of detective stories: the first one with Reginald De Puyster, a sophisticated detective similar to Philo Vance; the second one with his more famous character, Lieutenant Valcour; Colin Starr, who appeared in four stories in the *Strand Magazine* during 1940/41; and Detective Bill Duggan, who appeared in three stories in 1956/57. The Bill Duggan stories include his most famous short work, "Malice in Wonderland" (which loaned its title to his 1958 hardcover short story collection).

Modern critics are rediscovering Rufus King's work. Mike Grost, on *Golden Age Detective*, features a long writeup of King, stating: "King had a vivid writing style, with colorful characters, events, and images. He was clearly a born writer."

www.ingramcontent.com/pod-product-compliance
Lightning Source LLC
Chambersburg PA
CBHW020140180626
46810CB00004B/1648